My Heartless Valentine

Written by Michelle Mackenzie

Chapter One

The year had barely begun before the stores were pushing out the valentine's gifts on to the unsuspecting customers, who wanted nothing more than to do their weekly shopping. Of course, the corporation wanted nothing more than money, and lots of it.
Claire, however, wasn't shopping for food or the usual bakewell tart. No. With the start of the year she had, she was going to need something else.

The police force had always been hard work, though, lately, she had been working a little harder than she used to. Her partner retired, and left her in the lurch. It wasn't his fault, she supposed. Once you reach the point of being shot so many times, they don't usually think along the lines of "what the heck, it's just one more time". No. This time was the last time, and they sent him off to retirement along with a basket of muffins and a nice shiny watch. Graham didn't wear watches, and thanked his colleagues through gritted teeth. And now, Valentine's day was just around the corner, and she was being reminded of the fact everywhere she went. If she had a date with mr tall, dark and handsome from work, she wouldn't have minded so much. But since he didn't even know she existed, she decided to settle for a good book and a nice bottle of rose.

She glazed over the shelves in the middle of the
off-licence store, in search of her favourite brand. It
took a little longer to find it this time round. The
staff had rearranged the isles. Again.

Finally finding the wine she was looking for, she
reached down and grabbed two bottles before
carrying them over to the cashier.
The cashier was a young woman with short blonde
hair, and wore rose-gold rimmed glasses. She took
the wine from her, and glanced up briefly at Claire's
face.
She scanned the bottles without comment.
Claire frowned. "How old are you?" she asked,
pulling a folded note from her purse.
"Twenty-one," the woman replied, and shoved the
drinks into a carrier bag.
She didn't look a day over eighteen.
"That'll be eighteen dollars," the cashier said.
"I don't suppose you have an ID on you?" Claire
frowned. "You look a little younger."
"No," she snorted. "I'm working. I'm the one that
asks for ID."
"It's just for my peace of mind. You know the rules,
right?"
"Who are you, the police?" the cashier replied,
getting defensive.

"Yes, actually. So, if you please? I'd like to see some ID. Minors aren't allowed to sell alcohol to anyone, whether they're adults or not."

She huffed and pushed a button under the till. "Someone will be down shortly."

She leaned over, turning her attention to the next person in the line. "Next please!"

Claire looked behind her, frowning, and checking their items for contraband. Vegetables, meat and dairy lined the till belt. Satisfied that there was nothing else she couldn't sell, she nodded and stepped aside.

It was almost ten minutes before the supervisor stepped up. "What seems to be the problem?" he demanded.

"This lady doesn't want me to sell her the alcohol, and I don't have ID," she explained simply. "Says I look too young. Vouch for me, please?"

He frowned, then glanced towards Claire's serious expression. "That's fine," he replied, softening his tone.

"I just wouldn't be comfortable making assumptions," she explained.

"It's fine. We get it all the time. Would you feel better for me to sell you the wine instead?"

Claire nodded, though reluctantly. "I also will need to see her ID. If she is underaged, then you would be

3

breaking the law - and as her manager, you would be liable for it."

He cleared his throat. "Yes, that is a valid point. Let me tell you what. I'll scan this, and then we'll go and get her ID. I'm sure Shannon can cover for five minutes."

"Who's Shannon?" she pushed.

"Shannon is my colleague. Don't worry, she's past thirty."

Claire relaxed a little and nodded. She passed the money to the manager, watching as he scanned the bottle of wine.

"Now," he said confidently. "Let's get you some reassurance."

"Britney, can you swap with Shannon for a moment?" he asked.

She stopped, mid-scan, as she held a loaf of bread. "What?"

"Just for a moment," he told her.

She huffed again, and placed the bread in a bag, and stepped aside for Shannon to slide into her place. "What now?"

"Britney, can you please show the lady your ID."

"Why?"

"Because, if you are selling alcohol underage, it affects us all - not just you."

She looked at Claire and her Manager with a flat expression. "This is a joke. It's in my bag."

They waited, watching for her to go and get it. She didn't move.

"Where is it?"

"In my locker."

The manager pointed towards the far end of the shop. "Let's go then, and give the lady some assurance that you're ok. It's just for her peace of mind."

Britney opened her locker and pulled out her purse, then handed her card to her manager with disgust.

"This is so age-ist," she complained. "Just because I look good for my age, and she doesn't."

Claire's mouth dropped open. She was about to comment on her manners, but the manager beat her to it.

"That is enough, Britney," he interjected. "This is an officer, who had a valid concern. And looking at this, so do I."

"Why? I'm twenty one, so it's fine."

He cleared his throat. "She had a concern, and looking at this, so do I."

"What did I do now?" she demanded.

He pointed towards the expiry date on the driving licence. "You tell me. How did you get here?"

"I drove here, obviously."

He looked like he wanted to cry. "Wait one moment, please."

They watched as he headed back towards Shannon, and then returned with a sour expression on his face.

"Take a look at your licence expiration date," he repeated.

She sighed, and looked down at the small four digit number, then cussed. "Dang," she muttered. "Am I in trouble?"

"Yeah," Claire replied, half apologetically. "Because you just admitted to driving here, and you don't have a valid licence."

"But I passed my test!" she argued.

"True," Claire said, acknowledging her achievement. "But, your licence has run out, meaning you drove without one. I'm gonna have to take you in."

"Now?! I'm working! What about my car? I can't just leave it here."

Claire shook her head, already wishing she stayed home. "It won't stay here. It'll be impounded, until you get a renewal."

"How long will that take?"

Claire shrugged. "Depends on the day to be fair. Get it done quickly, and it shouldn't be an issue. Until then, I'm afraid you're stuck with a fine and some points on your licence."

Her face paled, and she groaned again. "More points? At this rate, I may as well not bother!"

"More points?" she frowned, arching an eyebrow.

"Uhh! Yeah, forget I said that."

Claire closed her eyes, reminding herself that she was off duty. She was here for the wine and nothing else.

"Just... don't drive home," she told her.

After Britney agreed, and placed the car key into her locker, Claire left the building. She just hoped that the young woman would heed her warning, she wouldn't be given another chance again.

Claire placed her wine in the fridge and went to take her spot on the sofa in front of the television. Of course, Valentine's Day was being advertised and promoting flowers, chocolates, restaurants and wine. She scoffed, rolling her eyes at the prices being jacked up for the occasion. She switched off the television defiantly. "I'm going to bed," she muttered.

Chapter Two

Valentine's Day. The day she was dreading. The sun shone unforgivably through the glass, flooding the bedroom with light. Claire groaned, pulling the pillow over her head.

The alarm vibrated beside her, the teeth-grating noise that reminded her of dying crows. She sighed, defeated, and switched off the alarm and slowly climbed out of bed. The sight in the mirror didn't help, giving her the appearance of a zombie with who had just been electrocuted - the only reasonable explanation of why her hair stuck out in each direction. The coffee maker was already running when she made her way into the kitchen. Her favourite mug was already sitting beside the machine, waiting to be filled. A habit she required after countless smashed cups that she had dropped. Finally sitting at the table, her eyes glazing over the newspaper, she took a sip of her black coffee, appreciating the bitter flavour.

Her phone rang. She was tempted to ignore it. But after the fifth ring, she answered. "Morning," she grumbled.

"Good morning!" a gruff voice replied.

She blinked, immediately recognising the desolate tones of the tall dark and handsome colleague she'd been drooling over.

"Uh, Hi. Mark? H-Happy Valentine's Day."

"Yeah, you too. Speaking of which, someone likes you. They left you a present."

Claire frowned. "What? A Present?"

"Yeah, it's in a paper bag sitting on your desk. We have no idea how it got there - it was here before any of us arrived. We suspect the Janitor, but he swears he has no idea where it came from."

She knew the Janitor, and he was often kind, but she doubted that he liked her in that sense.

"All right," she sighed. "I'll come on in, but only because we don't know what's in there."

He thanked her for the time, and hung up. She rolled her eyes, looking again at her reflection, stunned. "A gift for me?" she questioned herself. "Probably more like a prank." Reluctantly pulling on her clothes, and after tugging a brush through her hair, she applied her makeup and sighed. She looked again at her reflection. Only the shadows beneath her eyes betrayed her otherwise tired expression, other than that, she looked ready to go. She groaned, grabbed her keys and left, already regretting her decision.

She pulled up to the station half an hour later, her colleagues greeting her with excited smiles. "Come on, guys," she chuckled. "We don't even know what it is yet!"

She took off her coat and casually scanned the far end of the room to where her desk was. There it was, sitting in the centre of her desk. At first glance, it seemed to be a medium-sized paper bag, rolled at the opening. She cleared her throat, not to appear too eager. Her colleagues followed behind her as she weaved through the desks towards her own. She held her breath, unrolled the bag and froze.

"Who's idea is this?!" she demanded, pressing her palm to her chest, heaving. "This is sick! This ain't funny, y'all!"

Her colleagues looked at her with confused faces, mumbling to each other. "What are you talking about? What's in it?!"

She cleared her throat, and delicately placed her hand inside the bag before pulling out a transparent plastic bag, covered with blood. Inside, sealed shut, was the remains of a heart. The room turned into a vacuum, a soundless void. No one dared to draw breath. "Well?" she demanded, breaking the eerie silence. "Who did this?!"

No one had an answer. Confused faces exchanged looks of concern to one another.

"So no one knows who put this on my desk?!" she demanded. "No one?!"

"What is it?" Mark asked, stepping to her side.

She held the plastic bag in the air for all to see. "It's half of a heart," Claire replied. She frowned, pulling it closer to her face for a better look. Then, dropped it back into the paperbag, feeling nauseous. "What's worse, I think it's human. So, someone literally gave me a heart. Three questions."

"What. The. Fuck?" Mark listed.

"Yes, but also: Where's the rest of it? Who does the heart belong to? And..." she took a deep breath.

"The biggest question: Where's the rest of the body? Because someone out there is missing a heart."
"Ooh. Yeah. Good point," Mark mused, growing serious. "Happy Valentine's Day!" he said weakly.

Claire shot Mark a glare, unamused by his attempt at making light of the situation. This was no laughing matter. It was only a matter of time before someone would be reported missing, if they weren't already. Among the questions she voiced to her colleagues, it lead to ones that needn't be asked. Who took it, and why send it to her? She passed the heart to the coroner with a grim expression. "I'm afraid this is all you have to work with for now, at least until we find the rest of the body."
The coroner laughed nervously, "well, it looks like we've got a heartless valentine this year. Definitely a first," she mused.
"It seems so," she replied. "And with someone else's heart in our hands. I just hope we find out who the heart belongs to."
Her gaze drifted to the window, lost in thought. If this was a play for her attention, who knows how far the killer would go. A chill ran down her spine, and she shuddered.

The coroner placed the heart remains on the scales in front of her. "The weight and the size of this heart suggests a middle-aged person," she stated. She moved the heart on to the slab table, and changed her latex gloves for a set of clean ones. "I'll autopsy the heart, but I'm not sure what information I can get from it."

"Maybe the time of death, or at least, the cause of it?"

She sighed, leaning in. Then cleared her throat. "Judging by the colour, I'd estimate it at around two days, maybe. Cause of death is a little clearer. Your victim was stabbed. The shape of the tip of the knife is still visible."

"Couldn't that be from breaking the heart into two?" Claire asked, cocking her head to one side.

"If the cut was a little closer to the split, yes. But not in this case. There's enough of a gap for me to see, the victim was stabbed with a fish knife - noted by the wide tip and the serrated edge."

"I see," Claire gasped. She couldn't see of course, all she could see was the cut edges dorn the organ as it was split into two.

"Odd question," the coroner said, speaking up. "But, what happened to the other half?"

"W-what?" Claire asked, confused.

"The other half. This had been clearly cut into two. So, who has the other half of the heart?"

Claire froze before replying. "I'm going on a hunch and say the murderer has it." She pressed her hand to her stomach, feeling the familiar wave of nausea again. "I hate valentines," she muttered.

It didn't take long for the Captain to get wind of what was happening. He walked through the door, with his glasses perched on the tip of his nose. She never understood why he insisted on looking over them, when they were clearly meant for using. She pressed her lips together, watching as his eyes glazed over the gift.

"Any thoughts?" he asked, as though she would already have suspicions. She didn't and could only hazard a guess.

"Uh, well... someone obviously wants our attention. It may not have been intended for me - more than likely it was placed on a random table. Now that they have our attention, we'll look into who has been reported missing and maybe get a blood type match from the organ. That should narrow down our search, at least."

"Good, good," he said, half listening. "Go with Mark and start asking around the perimeter. Someone must have seen something."

Since it was early, she doubted it. "Yes sir," she replied. At least one thing came from this disaster - she got to work tall, dark and handsome. She said goodbye to the coroner and walked out, holding her head up high.

Chapter Three

The street was quieter than she had hoped. The day was long and she could do nothing but wait for the results. If the heart was human, that would be a whole can of worms she doesn't not want to endure. Sometimes, she wondered why she became a cop. It was a thankless job, and no one appreciates the fact that she puts her life on the line every week. Lately though, more days than not.

Please, she heard someone mutter. "Please, I just need one more day."

She could relate. One more day for bills. One more day for work. One more day off. The world lived off hoping for that one more day. It never came.

"On the news today, a body is discovered without a heart."

Claire blinked. Could this be her victim?

"A donor was at the hospital today who had died on the table with some uncertain circumstances. But when the doctors went to harvest the heart from the donor, they were surprised to find out someone had beat them to it, and had ripped their heart out of their chest. Whoever it was, it seems they didn't want the heart to go to the woman who was waiting for it, despite all checks to say it was safe. Was someone bitter with the woman, or did the heart belong to someone else? More of this, after the break."

Claire switched off the television, and grabbed herself a glass of wine. Perhaps she needed to take a break from being inside four walls. She drained the glass in one. She needed a distraction. She sighed, and then decided the next best thing was to maybe go to the pub. At least there, she thought to herself, she might find someone who would spark some ideas. Besides, it was valentines day, and the thought of being alone sucked.

The nearest bar was the Jackson family bar. Claire walked up to the main door and pushed it open. She was immediately greeted by the distinct smell of stale beer, vomit and cigarette smoke.
"Evening," she said, greeting the stouty looking bartender. "I'll have a whiskey please?"
He grunted an acknowledgement and took the twenty note before sliding the glass towards her. He kept the change, not that it was a lot. Drinks were expensive now, thanks to the cost of living crisis. The government say its a new thing, but the cost of living had been a thing for more than ten years. If they hadn't solved the crisis, it's not a crisis, it's life. She took a large mouthful of her drink, pulling a face. The whiskey burned the back of her throat.
"That's a strong drink for a pretty lady like yourself," came a hoarse voice. She turned around, finding a man with stubble cheeks. He had thick black wavy

hair, and a tight black shirt on, pulled down over his blue denim jeans. As much as he tried to make it look like he'd just thrown on an outfit, it was obvious he picked the shirt that revealed the most. She cleared her throat, taken aback.

"Excuse me?!" Claire questioned.

"The name is Harris," he replied. "Xander Harris."

"Claire," she said, introducing herself briefly. She didn't bother giving him her family name.

"Well, Claire," he said, helping himself to a seat beside her, "How come you're spending Valentine's Day alone?"

She looked at him for a hard minute, questioning whether he was stupid or whether he was just making conversation.

"I don't know," she sighed. "I guess I'm just unlucky."

He paused, making no attempt at hiding him, checking her out. His eyes travelled up her body.

"Unlucky? Maybe the universe was saving you for me."

She shuddered and took another mouthful of her whiskey. "Yeah, I don't think so," she replied.

He stood up, his expression soured. "Oh, too good for me, pretty lady?" he snapped. "You're all the same. A tease. Coming in here and--"

Another man walked over. Clean shaven, holding out a glass of red wine towards her. He planted a kiss on her cheek, cutting in between Xander and herself. "I am so sorry I am late, darling. I got held up. Forgive me?"

Claire blinked, trying to catch up with what was happening. She gasped, and then smiled, stretching her arms out to welcome him with a hug.

"Oh my god, I thought you stood me up!" she exclaimed happily. "Is that drink for me?"

"Of course," he replied, passing her the glass. "I couldn't very well be late and be empty handed; that'd be rude."

Xander, who suddenly looked foolish stormed off, and slammed the door behind him. Claire breathed a sigh of relief. "Thanks for the rescue."

He laughed. "You're welcome. I'm sorry I couldn't get here sooner, the bartender was extremely busy."

Claire smiled. "It's fine. I'm just thankful that you came when you did. I really didn't want to have to get into it with him."

"Glad to be of help."

She went to hand back the wine, smiling. "Thanks for this."

"Oh, no," he replied, pushing her hand away, "that really is for you. I'm going to sit..." he pointed towards the direction of the table at two tables across from them "over there. So, if you need me, that's where I will be."

She thanked him again and smiled. "Thank you. Means a lot."
He nodded, and stood from his chair. "Happy Valentine's Day, Claire." he said, and smiled.

She was once again alone, and feeling a little more at ease knowing that at least someone was watching her back. She sipped at her drink, swirling the red liquid around the glass, the way the professional wine tasters do before taking the tiniest sip. She, however, was not a professional taste-tester, and instead took a large swig from her glass. It was dry and fruity, not at all like vinegar like her previous experience in drinking wine. Then, she let out a loud, unladylike sigh of satisfaction.

After she had finished her drink, she felt a little more relaxed. Her mind began to wonder to the investigation and the paper bag on her desk. She still could not believe that someone had sent half a heart. She cringed, pushing the imagery out of her head. There were so many questions about what was going on, and she had no answers. Why half a heart? Was it human? Why was it in a sealed plastic bag? Did it have anything to do with the donor, or the patient the heart was originally meant to go to? She pinched the bridge of her nose, and signalled the bartender for another glass of wine. It was going to be a long night, and there would be no answers until morning at the very earliest. Until then, she scowled herself. "I need to calm the fuck down." If only she knew how.

She eventually made it home, after what seemed like a couple of drinks. In reality, two hours had passed and she had more than a few. The street spun around her, with no sign of stopping. She held the wall as she walked, and leaned on every lamp and post until she finally made it home. Cars passed her were very few and far between, giving the nightlife and eerie feel to the silence. Even the birds had stopped, leaving her to fumble for her keys.
After sliding the key into the lock, she clicked it open and stepped inside. The hall was dark. The narrow halls closed in on her. Her heart pounded. She closed the door behind her, and slid her hand over the wall until she could find the light.
There, by the door frame, she could feel the plastic frame. CLICK.
The light illuminated the hallway, flooding it with light, and bringing her home into life. Pictures of her family filled the room, full of memories of her past holidays.
Claire dropped her bag down on the floor and made her way to the bedroom. Turned the light off once more and fell into bed. She was asleep the moment her head touched the soft plump pillow.

Chapter Four

The morning came with an unforgiving glare. She groaned, covering her eyes. The alarm sounded in her ears. She tapped the snooze button and sat up in bed with a groan. She could already smell the coffee brewing, welcoming her to the day. The coffee machine was the best thing she had purchased in years. Well, that, and her favourite mug.

Waiting for the coffee to finish being prepared, she stumbled into the bathroom, washed her face and got dressed. The alarm sounded again. She switched it off and headed for the kitchen, where the coffee machine was finally finished in preparing her drink. Timing was everything. She poured the contents into her thermal mug, screwed on the lid and sat herself on her stall. Just as she was about to take a mouthful of her coffee, her phone began to ring. The coroner's face lit up the screen.

"Hello, Carol. Do you have any news for me?"
"I wouldn't be calling in this ungodly hour if I didn't," she replied.
"All right," Claire said, smiling. "Please, tell me that it isn't human and this is something for animal welfare to deal with."
"I'm afraid I can't do that. You were right. The heart came from a middle aged human. And from what blood I could get from it, it was from a middle-aged male."

Claire groaned. "I was hoping it wouldn't be. Do you think it came from the donor mentioned on the news?"

"Probably. I would have to get access to the donor's body to find that out though."

"All right," she sighed, closing her eyes. She was already wishing she could go back to bed. "I'll make some calls and see what I can do. In the meantime, though, I'd treat this as a murder."

Those are the words she prayed she wouldn't hear, especially around this time of year. "Ok," she stated, holding up her head. "Then I guess, we better get the plastic bag checked for fingerprints. Hopefully, it'll give us something to work with. I'll call Mark as well, and give him an update. Once we get confirmation that the heart is from the donor, we'll have a good place to start the investigation: beginning with, who doesn't want the patient to have the heart in the first place. And who else had access to the body."

The coroner hung up with the phone, leaving Claire alone with her thoughts. Who would she call for that kind of information? The nurses. She had been working in Homicide for almost fifteen years, and she had never had to deal with a case like this before. She missed the regular find of the body, laying on the ground somewhere, whole. None of these missing organs bull. She sighed. Correction, the body wasn't missing, they just weren't in the same place. Still, the timing of the case didn't sit right with her, and she couldn't help but to wonder if this had been done before. She dialled Mark's number and waited for him to answer the phone.

"Yo," he replied, as though he had been expecting his mates to call.

"Yo," Claire echoed back. "We gotta work. The heart came back. It's human, and belonged to a middle-aged male. Carol is going to check the blood type of the donor, and find out if the heart belongs to him. But whilst we're waiting on that, we're gonna need to dig into something."

"Wait wait wait. You were right about it being human and middle aged?"

"Yes," she replied. "So, get your arse into gear. We have work to do. Carol says to treat it like a murder. So, let's do our jobs. We need to know if there are any other organs missing from the donors. If it's a black market gig, then we'll have a starting point."

"And if it is not?" he questioned.

"Then, it's an isolated incident and won't need to be looking for extra bodies. And whoever took the heart, either wanted it to be found by us as a whole, or was a sick gift. So, let's make sure we're thorough."

"All right, all right," he huffed. "I'm on my way."

She sighed, hanging up the phone and glanced down at her thermal mug of coffee. Best buy ever. She grabbed her coat and her keys, before walking out of the house.

As she approached her car, something caught her eye on the windshield. A small business card was tucked beneath her wiper. She looked around for a sign of anyone hanging about. The row of houses were still. The cars were all off, parked along the sidewalk. She frowned. Whoever had left it there was gone. She grabbed the card and turned it over. Simon Kindle. Under the name was a phone number and a small message written in pen. "Happy Valentine's Day. I'm glad you got home safe."

She frowned. Did her knight in shining armour follow her home? She slipped the card into her pocket, shaking her head. She had bigger issues to deal with. She opened the car door and climbed inside, before driving off towards the station. A twisted knot sat at the pit of her stomach the whole way there.

At the station, Mark was waiting outside when she arrived.

"Took you long enough," he scowled. "I thought you would be here already."

She frowned, and climbed out of her car. "I was called from home too," she replied curtly. "So, unless you wanted me to come to work in my night clothes, be thankful it only took me about fifteen minutes to arrive. You, however, live a lot closer. Otherwise, I would suspect that I would still be waiting for your arrival."

He made his way to the entrance in front of her and pulled open the door. "After you," he commented. Claire thanked him, gave him a smile and stepped inside.

Claire and Mark made their way towards the autopsy room where Carol was waiting. Just as they opened the door, she put the phone down with a shake of her head.

"It's just been confirmed. The heart belongs to the donor."

She blinked. "How did he die?" Claire questioned, wondering if it was indeed a murder or not.

"Unclear," Carol replied, shrugging her shoulders. "According to the family, he simply went to sleep and never woke up."

This bothered her. Something in her gut, shifting around like she was sitting on needles.

"Really? That's strange, right?"

"Not really. But that is why it's unclear. He had regular checks, and had regular visitors. But he died in his sleep all the same."

Claire fell silent for a moment. "Given the fact that half of his heart was sitting on my desk yesterday, I am going on the assumption and say this is highly suspicious. Can you get the donor's body to the autopsy table?"

She smiled at her, and gestured towards the door. "It's already on the way down. I came to the same conclusion. When I have done the autopsy, I'll have more information for you. Until then, you have your starting point. The family is waiting at the hospital for you."

"Thank you, Carol," Claire said, before walking out of the door.

Mark frowned, and followed behind her. "I think we're missing something," he announced, trying to keep up.

"Yeah? What's that?"

"Well, if we're treating this as suspicious, what happens to the patient who was waiting on the heart?"

Claire gave him a side-eye look and shook her head in dismay. That was one answer she really didn't want to give. Her looked at her and waited. She took a deep breath, stopped and turned to face him. "If there's no other heart available for the patient, then she goes back on the list... or she dies."

He looked at her, his expression turned to stone. He hardened his resolve. Transplant was a raw subject from him, and he rarely spoke of his mother. "Then, having killed the donor... if the patient dies, does the killer then be charged for two deaths, instead of one?"

Claire thought for a minute. "I think so. At least, that's the way it should be. But I will have to look into it...just to be sure."

He nodded in agreement. "It wouldn't be fair if he is only charged with the one death, rather than two."

Climbing back into the car, they made their way to the hospital. She sighed, and turned to face Mark with a confused frown. "Are you sure you'll be alright in this case?"

He nodded, and shrugged his shoulders. "I'll be fine. It's not like we're going to be visiting the same room as she was in. And if it gets too hard for me, then I'll step outside. But at the moment, I am ok." He paused for a moment, clicking his seat belt into place. "Thank you for checking though. Means a lot."

She nodded and restarted the engine. With everything that was going on, it was already beginning to look like the case was going to be long, tedious and complicated.

The hospital car park was packed. Getting a parking space was going to be a mission by itself. "Argh!" she grumbled, frustrated. "I'm just going to park in the middle of the road in a minute," she grunted. "Don't do that," Mark sighed. He pointed. "There, three cars down. Grab that one."

Without hesitation, she reversed left and pulled into the space. "Thanks," she said, feeling a little better.

"At least we won't have far to walk," he told her. Claire nodded but said nothing. It was just going to be that kind of day.

The family was waiting in the cafe, hugging their coffees with both hands.

"Hi there," Claire said in a soft tone. "I am so sorry for your loss. I'm here to talk to you about your husband. Are you ok to answer a few questions?"

The wife wiped a tear from her face with the corner of her sleeve. "Yeah. Do what you must. My day can't get any worse."

Claire cleared her throat. "Well, let's go and find a private room."

Mark pointed to the room across the hall. "In there will do."

The family glanced in the direction Mark pointed in, then slowly climbed to their feet.

They followed them into the room and took the first seat available.

"Sit down," Mark said, pulling out a seat.

Claire thanked him, and tucked herself in under the table.

"Lets start with his name: Just so that I have it on record."

"It's George. George Rocks." The wife teared up again. "He was such a gentle soul. I don't understand why this is happening."

"What you mean?" Mark asked, taking a seat beside Claire.

"Well, why would someone take his heart?"

Claire cleared her throat. "It may be more than that," she told her. She watched as the wife frowned, confused.

"W-What? What are you talking about?"

Mark leaned forward. "We have reason to believe that he was..." he searched for the right word "...helped to the end."

The wife stared at him, her vacant expression fixed on his.

"We think he was murdered."

"M-Murdered?" the wife echoed. Her face paled, her eyes went wide. "No. No no no, he passed in his sleep," she corrected them. "Don't start telling people he was murdered. He wasn't!"

"I'm sorry," Claire said, though she kept her tone firm. "But that is our theory at the moment. The only way we'll know for sure is if we investigate, but I am praying that it is not the case, but we have to be certain. You understand?"

"Of course I understand," she snapped. Her face became red and enraged. "Well, what is it that you need to know?" she demanded.

Claire took out her notebook. "Well, let's see... who was the last one to see him alive out of you all?" Claire's eyes scanned around the room for any sign of acknowledgement. "Are any of you the last one to leave the room? Or was it the nurse that was the last one out. Try to remember."

The wife thought for a moment, scratching her head. "Lets see... there was myself, then christine, david... then the last to leave for that night was... Michael, his wife Judith... and then the nurse... oh, what was her name...?" she tapped her chin, thinking. "What was it?!" She paused. They could see her racking her brains, trying to shake something loose. Her face scrunched up, thinking hard. Then, she snapped her fingers. "That was it! Tiara - I remember because her name sounded like Tia."

Claire jotted the name down, and looked around. There couldn't be many Tiara's in the hospital. The name was almost unheard of. She smiled, and then turned towards the rest of the family. "All right. So, tell me about the donation. How long has he been an organ donor for?"

"Donor?" The wife looked more confused then before, if that was possible. Claire blinked, tapping the pen on her paper.

"Yes. How long ago did he agree to give away his heart?"

She stared at Claire and Mark, dumbfounded. "He didn't," she replied. "He's not a donor at all. What made you think he was?"

Claire grabbed the sheet from the foot of the bed, with all of his medical information printed on it. There at the bottom, the information they needed. She showed the wife. "See," she stated, pointing to the signature. "That's his handwriting, isn't it?" She squeezed her eyes, trying to make out the squiggle on the dotted line.

"It looks very similar," she said finally, and then shook her head. "But no. That isn't his signature."

"Are you sure?" Mark asked, interjecting himself into the conversation. "What makes you so sure?" She took out a form from her handbag and passed it over to Mark, pointing towards one of the letters.

"See there," she said, pointing to the letter e. "See how the tail flicks slightly at the end?" Claire frowned, and took a closer look at the signature. Then, placed it side-by-side to the medical form. Sure enough, the letter had a flick.

"It's a twitch," the wife explains. "He was diagnosed recently. I can't remember what it was. But his hand twitches when he isn't resting it on something. So, when he raises his hand to take the pen off the paper, he twitches a little, causing the flick at the end. The signature on the form doesn't have that."

Claire frowned. She needed to be sure. "Uh... I don't suppose you have other letters with his signature on it, do you?"

She sighed, then frowned as she dug back through her bag. She had a whole pocket of letters, crammed into a single section. Then, carefully, she pulled out her wedding certificate. "Would this do?"

Claire gasped. "Perfect," she said. There was no faking those. "Let me have a look?"

The wife handed over the certificate and held her breath. Claire held her breath with her, as she inspected the squiggly line on the bottom of the page. "There," Claire said, showing Mark. "He flicked here too. It's subtle but it is definitely there."

Mark shook his head in dismay. "Well, that makes it all very clear. Doesn't it," he stated.

Claire nodded her head. "Yeah, There is no question about it. Miss, your husband was murdered."

There was a long pause. "Why would someone give away his heart?" Claire asked, frowning.

Chapter Five

Nothing about this case made sense. Worse, the investigation had only just begun.

"If he isn't here as a donor, we should go further back. What exactly did he come into the hospital for?"

"He came in as a precaution," his wife explained. "He fell off the ladder changing a light bulb and banged his head. He insisted he was fine, but I told him--"

She stopped, and her face paled. Her expression of despair changed into one of horror. "This was my fault," she gasped. "If I hadn't told him to come in, he'd still be alive!"

"You can't think like that," Mark told her softly. "You didn't know."

The wife stared off into nothingness, lost in the abyss of despair. There would be no more answers coming from her any time soon. She gently thanked the family for their time and left the room, leaving the wife and the siblings in their grief.

Claire frowned, climbing back into her car. She pulled out her notes, and placed them on her lap, thinking. "A heart turns up on my desk, belonging to a donor-who never signed up to be a donor, and he was murdered. So... it's not the case of the heart being stolen and refusing to give up the heart.

Someone targeted him specifically, killed him, and literally ripped his heart out of his chest. This took a lot of planning. It took a lot of time."

Mark agreed, sighing as he leaned back in his chair. "It had to have come from someone he knows. If he had on-going medical issues, I'd suspect maybe a doctor… but coming in because he bumped his head? It seems unlikely."

Claire groaned, dropping her head back against the headrest of the driving seat. "You're right. It had to be someone they knew. It had to be one of them."

She thought for a moment. Without a motive, there wouldn't be a lot to go on. And that still didn't explain why it ended up on her desk, in half!

"Let's look into their finances. Maybe something will come up."

Claire massaged her temples. "I should not have woken up today. I should have stayed in bed."

"Then the killer would be roaming the streets with no one knowing what they had done," Mark argued.

He had a point, she supposed.

"Fine," she huffed. "Let's go back to the autopsy. Maybe Carol will have something more for us to go on. Like, possibly, a time of death. And if we're lucky, something to indicate what killed him before his heart was ripped out."

She pushed the door open. Carol was at the far end of the room, washing her hands in a small sink.

"Come on in," she called out, looking over her shoulder.

"Do you have news?"

"Now that I have the whole body? Yeah. And there's... there's a lot."

Nothing surprised her at this point. "I don't doubt it. This whole case is a lot. What have you got?"

She handed the detective a handful of sheets.

"What's this?" Claire frowned, waving the paper.

"It's my findings," Carol explained. "I told you, it's a lot."

"All right. Time of death?"

She cleared her throat and sat down at her desk, looking at the digital file on her computer.

"According to the doctors, he died around seven in the evening. It was almost ten before they realised his heart was missing," she began. "But, now this is a weird bit. I put the time of death at three in the afternoon. Which leaves four hours of the victim being dead before anyone calls it in. The whole time he was 'sleeping', he was already dead."

Claire frowned. "Just how much of a deep sleeper is he?"

Carol shrugged. "I don't know. But going by the sinuses, the lack of silence should have been a clue."

"What do you mean?" Mark asked, stepping towards the body, as though he might be able to see something himself.

"His sinuses were small," she declared, raising an eyebrow. Carol sighed, looking at their blank expression on their faces. "He was a snorer."

"Ooh. So the lack of snoring would have been unusual?"

"Try unheard of," she replied in a matter of fact tone. "And the fact that they didn't check, meant he was either alone in the room for those four hours and no one checked on him, or they already knew he was dead."

"This case!" Claire cried out exasperated. "It's one thing after another!"

Claire walked around the halls, thinking to herself. He had been murdered. His heart was left on her desk. But... why? What did the killer want ? Her? Is her heart next?

She made her way to the pub, needing a break from the case. She needed to breathe. Since it was barely the afternoon, and it was only her lunch break, she ordered herself a cola without the added alcohol or rum.

"Long day?" a familiar voice said, greeting her.

She turned to face him. She smiled, immediately recognising the voice of the guy who saved her from the creep the night before.

"Oh hey," Claire said smiling, greeting him with a hug. "What are you doing here?"

"I volunteer here on the weekends," the man replied.

She laughed lightly and sat down at the first empty table she came to. The pub was already bustling with customers, filling the room with a hum of conversation. The familiar smell of beer from the night before still lingered, though she could now also make out the familiar stink of Bleach.

"Long day then?" he repeated, still waiting for an answer.

"Yeah," Claire replied with a sigh. "But I'll be alright. I'm just gonna take my lunch break and then get back to work."

He gave her a brief nod and walked away from the table, noticing a man waving an empty glass in the air. "I've gotta go, it looks like I'm being summoned."

She laughed and watched as he approached the man with the waving glass.

Returning to her brief lunch break, she was just about to bite into a sandwich when a chair was pulled out beside her.

"Hello again, pretty lady," he said with a sneer.

She sighed, rolling her eyes. "Hello, Mr Harris," she greeted. "Have you come to apologise for yesterday's behaviour?"

He stood behind his chair and scoffed. "Apologise? For what?"

"For being obnoxious," she told him firmly. "I take that as a no?"

"Listen here, you came to find me. Don't deny it." She watched as he swayed side to side on his feet, still drunk. Or perhaps, drunk again, she wondered. Was he ever sober? It seemed unlikely. Perhaps, a brief moment of sobriety before he returned to chugging down his next drink.

"Leave her alone, Xander!" came the familiar voice again.

She smiled, pleased that her saviour was still watching her back. She took a large swig of her cola, casting her eyes down at the tiny bubbles, pressing themselves against the surface of the cold glass. Mark would be having coffee in the cafeteria, she told herself. Not sitting in the bar, as she was. Claire felt a pang of guilt. Perhaps it was time to leave, and give up the drink. She placed the glass on the bartender's table and slid the note towards them.

"Thanks for the lunch," she said, smiling. Taking a last look around the establishment, and the dewy eyes of the lost souls stuck there, Claire walked out and breathed in the fresh air. It was time to get back to work, starting with the victim's workplace. If there were problems at home, work was a good place to start looking.

Mark was standing by the main entrance of the station, smoking a cigarette when she arrived.

"Hey Mark. Ready to go and ask some questions?" she asked him with a smile.

He nodded, snuffing the cigarette out on the wall behind him. She frowned, watching as the ash smeared against the brick, embedding itself into the grooves of the brickwork.

"What?" he asked, frowning, staring at her.

"Unbelievable," she muttered.

"What?!"

She cleared her throat. "That's someone's wall," she stated in her matter of fact tone.

"And?"

"And," she pressed on, "you just dug your cigarette into it."

He looked at her, expressionless, waiting for her to make her point.

"And?"

She took a deep breath, then exhaled. She needed to approach this differently.

"I'll tell you what. I'm going to spark up a cigarette, and then dig my lit cigarette into your nice white front door. And maybe stamp it out on your welcome mat."

"No-wait, what?" he blinked, grasping for words. "Why? Why would you do that?"

"Do what?" she replied in her most innocent tone.

"Why would you put out a cigarette on my stuff?"

"You just did. What's the difference?"
He spluttered his words, but they failed him. He
hung his head in defeat. "Fine, you win. I won't use
the walls any more."
"Good," she stated. "Now, let's go catch ourselves a
killer - and maybe find out why he put it on my desk
in the first place."

Chapter Six

The victim worked in an office, over-seeing the
mundane tasks of filing away paperwork and
restocking the printers.
Claire looked around the office, at the grey walls and
chairs, and the staff staring numbly at their
computer screens.
"Excuse me!" Claire asked, raising her voice over the
humming of machines. "I would like to speak to the
manager!"
The room fell silent, other than the faint sounds of
the computer fans, still whirling in the background.
"Says who?" a voice demanding. It was a small
woman with squared thick framed glasses.
"We do," Mark replied, showing his badge. Claire
flipped out her badge, holding it beside his. "We're
here about one of your co-workers. He went by the
name of George Rocks."

The manager pushed her glasses up against her face. "George isn't here today," she reported in a matter-of-fact tone. "Is he in some kind of trouble?" Claire frowned, and looked around. "I would say so, yes. What do you know about him?"

The manager smiled. "Delightful," she said, almost giddy. "It's about time! I knew that goody-two shoes persona was all an act. What'd he do? Steal? Burglary? Secret identity--no wait, was he a pirate?"

"What?!" Claire gasped, breaking the manager's eager rambling. "No. None of those."

"Oh," she sighed, making no effort to hide her disappointment. "What kind of trouble is he in then?"

"The worst kind," Mark told her, irritably. "He's dead."

"What? No. That can't be, we saw him just last week and he was fine!"

Claire cleared her throat. "Yeah, that's a thing about murder - you generally don't expect it. So, can we talk somewhere or do you want this to be a group discussion?"

The manager blushed and pointed towards a door on the left. "That room there will do. I'm Minerva by the way..."

Claire walked in behind Minerva and Mark, closing the door firmly behind her.

"Now," she said, hardening her tone. "What can you *really* tell us about George Rocks."

"Not much in all honesty," she replied defensively. "He was always a goody two-shoes, as I've stated before. He was one of those people who would hold doors open, stand when you leave the table... he even, at one point--" she paused, her face twisted in disgust, "he even paid for someone else's shopping because a *stranger* didn't have enough."

After it was clear Minerva could tell them nothing more, they called in the next co-worker. "James Darwin?"

A tall slender man stepped forward, brushing his blonde hair to one side. He strode towards them purposefully, as though he was walking down a runway, in the centre of attention.

"I am here," he announced, waving.

Claire rolled her eyes, side stepping him to allow room for his ego to enter the doorway.

"Great," she muttered under her breath. If there's one thing she couldn't stand, it was show-offs.

He sat himself down across from them, propping his ankle up with his leg.

"So, spill. What is really going on? You don't need to lie to me."

Claire blinked, stunned. "Lie?" she frowned. "What makes you think we'd lie?"

He shrugged, smirking. "Come on. I know. We pulled a pretty beasty prank on him last week.

There's no way he'd let us get away with it." He paused, as though a light bulb lit up in his head. "This is it, isn't it? To make us feel bad. Look," he said, not giving them a chance to respond, "it's not our fault he can't take a joke. I know he was upset, but this prank is just in bad taste."

Mark shook his head, and placed his hands on the table, palms down. He leaned in close, keeping his tone low. "Listen, I don't know what prank you pulled, but you need to hear me now. George Rocks is dead."

"Like, dead dead? As in really dead?"

Claire dragged her palms down her face. It was hard to imagine someone being so naive, yet be able to be in a work place such as an office.

Did he leave his brain cells outside? She shook her head, and pulled out a photograph. She had hoped she wouldn't be needing it. Then placed it in front of him.

"Does he look "dead dead" to you? Or do you think he might just be half dead?" she asked with thick sarcasm. "What do you think?"

His face paled, his eyes glued to the image of George, with his chest open.

"God!" he gasped, mortified. "It looks like something from that alien film!" He turned away, turning a little green. He took a deep breath, trying to calm himself, and looked again. "Why does he look like that? Why is his chest like that? What happened to him?!"

Mark let out a loud exasperated sigh. "Because he's dead!" he told him, frustrated. "Someone killed him, and ripped out his heart. So yeah, he's not looking his best. What would you look like after you've had your heart ripped out?"

James leaned back, his eyes tearing up. "What?" he said, his voice wobbling. "But why? Why would anyone do that?"

Mark leaned in, still glaring at him. "I don't know. You had no problem giving him a hard time, why don't you tell me."

James left the room with a vacant expression, white as a sheet. He barely looked at his colleagues as he returned to his desk, burying his head in his folded arms. Minerva stood in the corner of the room, watching helplessly as each person had their turn. After what seemed like a few hours, Claire thanked them for their time and left, with Mark following closely behind.

She sat in the car, taking in the brief silence before turning to her partner.

"There's no way someone goes out of their way to make that much of a performance out of the kindness of their hearts. Not in this day and age."

"What, you mean like a saint?" Mark questioned.

She nodded, her eyes gazing out in front of her, lost in thought.

"You're right," he agreed. "Which makes me think of something else."

She sighed and looked back towards him. She sucked in a breath, noting for the first time in a few days, how dark his brown eyes were. She let out a breath, reminding herself to remain focused.

"There's only one reason someone would put on a show like that."

"They have something to hide."

Claire nodded. "But it still doesn't explain how or why his heart turned up on my desk."

She only hoped that somewhere in this investigation, the case would make sense.

She thought for a moment, racking her brain for ideas. Frustrated, she settled on the obvious next move. "We need to go to his house. If there is anything he is hiding, it'll be there."

"What about his family?" he asked. "They'd see it, right?"

She shrugged. "Not really. Like alcoholics, those who have bigger secrets to keep, get really good at hiding it. So, take nothing for granted."

Time was fleeting, especially when there was so much to do. Claire stepped out of her car and faced the police headquarters darkened doorway, half hidden in shadows. She glanced down at the time, frowning. "Ten o'clock?" she read, gasping. "What happened to all the other o'clocks?"

Mark looked at her with a vacant expression. "We spent it questioning the office staff," he replied.

Claire shook her head. "But that was..."

"Three hours, and we left there forty five minutes ago."

"Oh..." she said, deflated. "I guess I hadn't been paying attention at the time. We'll call it a night and continue in the morning, then."

"Good idea," he told her. He waved briefly, raising his hand, and headed for his own car.

She looked around, observing the almost empty parking lot. There was still so much to do. "Fuck it," she muttered. She climbed back into the car and headed for the first place she could think of, and went straight to the bar. Perhaps, if she was lucky, Simon Kindle would be there.

She was sipping rum for almost an hour before she gave up waiting. She put down her fourth glass, and rose from her seat, just in time to see the entrance swing open. She held her breath, feeling hopeful. Stepping into the bar, a familiar figure loomed half hidden in shadows.

"Claire?" he asked, frowning.

She frowned back, shielding her eyes from the bulb's glare. "Mark? What are you doing here?"

"I couldn't relax," he replied, striding over towards her. "What about you?"

She shrugged. "I couldn't either, so I came to drink."

He leaned over slightly to one side, looking around her. Behind her, he could see a large clutter of empty glasses. "All yours?" he questioned.

She glanced back to her table where ten glasses were grouped together. "Yeah."

He cleared his throat, then ordered himself a beer, before glancing back towards her. "Want another?"

She shrugged. She wasn't gonna say no. "Sure," she replied, "why not."

"Another rum for my friend," he told the bartender, and slipped the server a tenner.

She followed him to a clean table, and grabbed the chair closest to her, watching as he gently placed the glasses down without spilling it.

"Nothing in this case makes sense," he grumbled.

She nodded. "Yeah, I know. I'm hoping that the visit back to the home will shed some light on the matter, but other than that - I'm just as clueless. There has to be a link somewhere that makes everything... not as complicated?"

"You think it'll be in the house?"

"I think," she replied tiredly, "it's a place to start."

"I thought work was the place to start?" he frowned.

She shot him a dirty look. "Usually we would have found something, and we did. It's not just as conspicuous as our normal findings. Rather than dirty secrets, or gossip, we found something else."

"Could we be wrong, though? Could he generally be a really nice guy?"

Claire laughed. "These days? I'd normally say no. But maybe someone took his people-pleasing as a threat..."

She sighed, listening to her own words. It just wasn't believable, even to her, despite it coming out of her own mouth.

"I suppose it's possible," Mark commented.

Claire frowned, baffled. "What?"

"I said, it's possible. What if someone thought he was flirting?"

She hadn't considered that. "It's a bit of an over-reaction," she said, mostly to herself.

"But likely. It's either that, or he's overcompensating for something darker."

"See, that's the thought I'm having. I suppose either could be the motive. Either way, we need to take a look inside his house. If there's anything sinister there, we need to know."

"Yeah, and then after, I propose we look into his male friends - or at least, the people who didn't like him."

Chapter Seven

Going by the reactions of the workplace, finding someone who wasn't a fan was going to be no easy task.

"Where do you look for something like that?" Mark asked. He shuffled his seat towards her.

Claire cleared her throat, trying not to stare at his bulging arms.

"Uh, um... well, I guess we can try the neighbours, and perhaps former workplaces. How long could he have been carrying on this performance?"

"Nah," Mark frowned, shaking his head. "No. I am thinking, we're looking too broadly."

"Oh? What do you suggest?"

"Men," he replied flatly. "Those girls he talks to, and be chivalrous to, they probably have boyfriends. Those are the ones we need to talk to. And maybe, find out who wants to rip his heart out in the process."

No matter how often she hears it, the words don't get any less surreal.

She switched on her engine, and turned on her fan. Having the car on, she automatically buckled herself in. Immediately after the click, her phone began to ring. They were being called back to the main room. There's another parcel on her desk, and this time, it wasn't wrapped.

She felt sick to her stomach. Claire turned towards Mark, who wasn't taking his eyes off her. "You've just had the one drink, right?" she asked.
He nodded. "Yeah, why?"
"There's something on my desk," she told him. Claire unbuckled her seatbelt. She had no idea why she was fastened in, she was in no fit state to walk, let alone drive. Yet, work had called her out. And according to the Captain, it couldn't wait.

Mark climbed into the driving seat, swapping over from Claire. He was taller than she was, and had to lower the seat down - ducking his head so he wouldn't hit the roof. After getting comfortable, they made their way down to the station. She watched him pull the car out of the driveway, her eyes transfixed on his defined muscles showing through his shirt. She could smell his cologne filling her vehicle, and all she could do was stare and breathe him in.

They pulled up to the station, with a single lamp lit up outside. It was barely enough to light the edge of the curb, as they approached the parking lot. Mark climbed out, then gave a helping hand to Claire, allowing her to lean on him as she made an attempt to keep her balance and appear somewhat sober. The tension filled the air, even as the doors opened before them, sensing their footsteps at the entrance.

The Captain, who was looking less than happy about being at work herself, was standing at the front of the room, greeting them the moment they stepped inside.

"It's for you," she stated, turning towards Claire with a questioning frown.

Claire frowned back. "How do you know it's for me? Is it just on my desk like last time or--"

"--not this time, it literally is sitting on your desk with a label clearly stating it is for you."

"By name?" Claire frowned, still not convinced.

"Yes. By name. Your first name."

She held her breath. Only a handful of people she worked with knew her by name. The rest of her co-workers only knew her by her family name and rank.

She approached her desk, hesitantly.

A small box was sitting in the middle of the table. It was plain, white, and seemingly made of cardboard. It was no wider than a small envelope, and no deeper than a couple of inches. She suspected it would be a tight fit for any limbs, unless it was a pinkie finger; but she doubted it.

She pulled on a pair of latex gloves, and opened the small box, holding her breath.

As the box unfolded before her, delicately trying not to damage any evidence, she gasped.

She snapped the box closed, frustrated. Her colleagues gathered around her like family on Christmas Day.

"Whose it from?" the Captain demanded.

Claire blinked, fanning herself before reaching for the card attached to the box.

"To Claire. To remind you of our time together," she read. She frowned again, turning the label over. That was it. "It doesn't say," Mark frowned. "How odd."

"What's in the box?"

She threw the box towards Mark, watching him catch it with both hands.

He opened it, frowning.

"It's... a key?" He looked up at Claire, hoping she'd enlighten him.

"Well, don't look at me!" she told him laughing, "I'm just as clueless."

The Captain held out a hand towards her. "Let me have a look at that."

Mark passed on the gift, as though he was throwing a penny into a pot.

"Well, it's obviously a key to a house. Are you seeing anyone?" she asked.

Claire shook her head. "I've talked to a guy once or twice, but not enough to get his attention. Saying that though, he did follow me home. But... I don't believe I told him I was a cop. And there was a guy who was rude... Xander Harris, I believe his name was."

There was a long pause, as they processed. "I think we need to find out what house this belongs to. I know a couple of people. Leave this with me. In the meantime, stick by Mark's side, and find out what you can about your heartless victim."

"You think I'm in some kind of danger?" Claire asked.

"We don't know," the Captain replied. "But we can't rule out that it's a trap either."

Claire couldn't argue with him, she knew he was right.

"Well, I'm not going to worry about that right now," she told him firmly. "First, we still need to go to the victim's house and find out whether or not the victim is hiding something."

"Not tonight you're not," the captain frowned. "I can tell you have been drinking. Though, I am aware that you were off duty, so I'm not pissed. But, I think it would be a good idea if you go home and sleep it off. You can go to the house in the morning. And I will call my associates in the morning about the key. Maybe we can find out what house it belongs to."

Claire nodded. "Good idea."

The next morning, Claire woke up nauseous. She pressed her palms against her stomach, trying not to throw up. Slowly, she got dressed and made her way into the kitchen. This time, she bypassed the coffee pot and instead poured herself a glass of ice water. Ten minutes later, she grabbed her handbag and a fresh bottle of water and slipped out of the front door. Her head was spinning, but with a killer on the loose, there was no time to feel sorry for herself.

Mark was already outside of the station, holding a costa coffee cup.
She groaned, feeling nauseous again.
"Are you alright?" he asked, smirking.
She nodded. "I'm fine. Just, keep the coffee away from me."
He laughed and climbed into the car. "I think I should drive," he stated.
"Yeah, good idea."
She shuffled over to the next seat, and cracked open a window.
She took a deep breath of the fresh air. Her head still spun. She groaned.
"Don't go being sick, will you?" Mark frowned, with a side-eyed glance.
"I won't," Claire told him, growing irritable. "Just, stop talking about it."

They pulled up to the house. The paint was peeling off the walls. The bushes were overgrown and the grass had grown to knee-level. Dandelion seeds gave the garden a blanket of grey, with flashes of yellow peering through the grass blades. She climbed out of the car, following behind Mark.

Claire looked around at the windows, watching for signs of movement. With everything appearing still, she reached out and pushed the doorbell, stuck against the door frame.

DING DONG! Blared through the street, startling her. Maybe the house was usually loud, or perhaps, she considered that maybe their hearing wasn't so good. She looked around, wondering if anyone else heard it.

"Do you think they're home?" Mark asked, turning towards her.

She glanced down at the time. It was nearing to Nine-fifteen. "Yeah," she replied. "It's still early."

The sound of footsteps approached the other side of the door. Claire smiled, noting that the hallway floor inside was either hard laminate or laid with a thin carpet. The door opened, revealing the grieving widow, with her hair sticking out wildly, and her shoulders hunched over.

"Yeah?" she asked, greeting them. "What do you want?"

"Hello," Claire said with a tired smile of her own. "Can we come inside?"

"Why?"

"Because we have some questions. And if possible, if we can look around. Maybe find something that might indicate who would want to kill your husband?"

She nodded, and stepped aside. "Come on in then, I'll grab a coffee, if you don't mind." She paused, and turned towards them, unsure. "Do you want one?"

Claire suppressed a groan and politely declined.

Mark smiled, holding out his cardboard costa cup. "Yes please, that would be great."

The smell of coffee filled the room within minutes. Claire's stomach turned and flipped, as she battled with the urge to be sick once again.

"Excuse me," she groaned. "Could I possibly use your bathroom?"

The widow nodded, pointing down the hall. "It's the door on the end."

Claire thanked her, and rushed down the corridor, clutching her stomach before stopping dead a few paces from the bathroom door.

"Oh my god!" the widow shrieked. "All over my carpet! What is wrong with you?!"

Claire groaned again. Her knees buckled, and she crashed to the floor on her hands and knees.

She hurled again.

"Stop it!" the widow cried.

Claire wanted to cry herself. Her face flushed red, mumbling out an apology. "Could you give me something to clean it up with?" Claire asked Mark, avoiding his gaze.

Mark nodded, and removed his jumper and shirt, then slipped his jumper back on before passing her his shirt.

She looked at him, confused. "Your shirt?"

"You've got sick down your top," he explained. I'll grab a handful of loo roll so you can clear the rest of it up, and I'll speak to the widow whilst you change."

Her lip wobbled, looking like she wanted to cry again. "Thank you," she replied tearfully. Then waited as Mark handed her a fistful of toilet paper. She scooped up her stomach contents, heaving. Just as she was clearing the last of the sick from between the floorboards, she paused. A panel of the flooring was lose. Using her fingernails, she dug up the loose panel and called Mark over.

"Mark?!" she cried out. "Come quickly!"

Inside beneath the flooring was a small metal box.

"What have you found?" Mark asked, looming over her.

"A box of some kind," she replied, pulling it from the small hole in the ground.

"Open it," the widow said, speaking up. She frowned, inching closer for a better look.

"Does it not look familiar to you?" Claire asked.

She shook her head. "No. I have never seen it before."

Claire cleared her throat, and carefully opened the container, and gasped.

"What is that?" the Widow questioned cautiously. Claire looked down, staring at the contents. "Secrets indeed," she muttered. Then pulled out a large stack of money, a passport with a different name on the front, and slowly, and very carefully, pulled out a gun.

"I am going to hazard a guess, but they're fake, right?" the widow said, though she didn't sound sure herself.

"No, no," Claire replied. "The money and the gun is very real."

"And the passport?"

She nodded. "It looks real, but I'm not a forgery expert. I'll have to get them to have a look for themselves. Either way, hiding large sums of cash, and having a gun--" she stopped, and checked the bullet chambers. "--Scratch that, make that a loaded gun, along with a passport of any kind, is bad news."

The widow shook her head. "What was George up to? I don't understand."

Claire shrugged. "I don't get it either. But if his name is really George, otherwise we're looking at," she looked down at the name on the card, "Jimmy Stones."

Mark sighed. "Either way, maybe we should look into the database. With this kind of hidey-box, he probably has a criminal record."

Claire agreed, and replaced the panel back into place. She passed the box to her partner, and excused herself to the bathroom.

Five minutes later, she emerged looking fresher, and wearing Mark's white shirt.

"It suits you," he commented, smiling.

Claire giggled, tucking her hair behind her ear. "Thanks."

He cleared his throat, and turned back towards the widow.

"You were saying?"

"Oh," she said, refocusing her attention on him. "I was saying, oh--that's right-- there was a man here just last month. He claimed to know my husband. He got peculiar about it when I asked him though. Shut up tighter than a clam, he did. I never did find out what he was here for."

"What did he look like?"

"Well," she said, casting her eyes to the side of the room, thinking. "He was tall, had dark curly hair... dark skinned..."

Claire felt nauseous again. It sounded like someone she knew, or thought she did. "Simon Kindle?" she asked, throwing the name out there.

Mark frowned, shooting her a questionable look. "Yes, that's it! Wait, but how did you know?"

Claire groaned. "Lucky guess," she replied weakly.

Mark followed her out of the room, his eyes fixed on her.

"You did not guess that. Tell me, how did you know? What aren't you telling me?"

Claire sighed, she had no choice in the matter. "A guy tried it on with me--quite rude. And this Simon guy came over and interrupted the attempt. He bought me a couple of drinks."

She paused, groaning again. She clutched her stomach.

"Not going to be sick again are you? I only have one shirt."

"No, it's worse than that," she said. "He followed me back one night."

"And?"

"So," she said, trying to keep calm. "He knows where I live."

Chapter Eight

"Please tell me you're joking?"

Claire shook her head. "I wish I was. He seemed like a nice enough guy, compared to Xander Harris, who was an ass..."

"I didn't know you were seeing someone," he grumbled.

Claire sighed. "Look, I wasn't "seeing" anyone. We talked. That's it."

"Anything else I should know?" he asked in an accusing tone.

"No," she replied. "But I'm thinking maybe we should compare handwriting to the other note? See if they're all from him?"

"Is that what you're hoping for?"

"Honestly, yes!" she cried out, frustrated. "Then we'd be that much closer to finding the killer!"

He gasped, horrified. "You liked him!"

"A little, yes! But I liked someone else more."

"Who? Another suspect?"

Claire couldn't believe her ears. "Are - Are you jealous?"

He scoffed. "No. But- Don't change the subject! Which other guy did you like? Maybe the dead husband - maybe that's why his heart was on your desk!"

She couldn't believe it. He *was* jealous!

"You!" she exclaimed angrily. "I liked you, you moron! But you didn't know I even existed until this case came along."

"Do you still like me?"

Shared stared at him, godsmacked. The one time he heard her, it had to be about *him*.

"Yes!" she replied bitterly. "But moments like this, I really wish I didn't."

"Why?" he asked, softening his tone.

"Because," she said, matching his tone. "You make me feel like a damned fool."

He groaned. "I'm sorry. I didn't mean to. I just don't like the thought of you putting yourself in harm's way."

A pure example of irony. "That's kinda my job," she reminded him. "But, thank you for your concern."

"Well, what do you want to do now?" he asked.

Claire shrugged. "The plan hasn't changed. We'llhead back to the station and check his identity against the database. We'll start with both of his names. If nothing comes up, then we'll run his photograph through the face recognition and maybe we'll get a hit there."

"And if not?" he asked, frowning.

She smiled. "Then, we'll cross reference Simon's credentials. Something is bound to pop up. Maybe we'll get lucky. If not, then it'll be a home visit. It's all we can do until the captain gives us something on that key."

Claire's stomach didn't feel much better, but at least she wasn't throwing up any more. Mark's shirt still smelled like his cologne, not that she minded.

"How long?" he asked, following her into the computer room.

"How long for what?" she frowned.

Mark dragged his feet on the ground, not meeting her glare.

"How long have you both been talking?"

She sighed. "Still on that? It's literally been a couple of times. First time was on valentine's day, and then again the day after. That was it. Nothing since. So, stop fretting. We have work to do. Besides, he might just be a bystander in all this."

"You don't believe that though?" he said, prompting her.

She let out a reluctant sigh. "No."

"How deep do you think he's in this?"

She tried not to think about it. She tried not to think how he knew where she lived. How long he'd been planning his approach. "Right in the middle," Claire told him flatly. "I just wish I saw the signs before."

She located the search bar on the database, and typed in George Rocks. The screen loaded, searching the files of millions of names. She crossed her fingers, though she wasn't sure what she wanted any more. Did she want him to be innocent in all of this? Of course. But, then, what of Simon? How did she feel about him? At this point, she wasn't sure of that either. Her gut twisted into a knot at the pit of her stomach. Thoughts haunted her. Had he entered her house when she wasn't there? Had he looked through her window at night? She shook her head. "Stop making yourself para," she muttered.

"What?" Mark asked, frowning.

"Oh. Nothing," she replied absent mindedly. "I was just talking to myself."

The loading screen stopped, and a picture appeared in front of them.

"George Rocks: Could not be found."

"Damn," she muttered. "We'll try another name."

She typed in the name on the passport. "Jimmy Stone."

Five seconds later, a profile came up on the monitor. She almost laughed.

"Jimmy Stone, Fifty-eight years old, and--"

"What?" Mark asked, leaning into the computer to read the screen.

"No way."

"Yeah. See, now I am confused."

She sighed, slumping back in her chair. "This case... It's caused nothing but headaches."

She rolled her eyes and scrolled down further on the screen. She shook her head and walked out of the room.

Mark frowned, even more confused. "Wait? Where are you going?"

He glanced back at the screen, trying to make sense of her sudden departure.

A name was written in bold. 'Claire Wittle.'

"Oh, shit," he cussed. He turned and raced after her, leaving the 'Donor' information page on the screen.

Claire was already in the car and fastened in when
he finally caught up with her.

"Where are you going?" he repeated.

"To find Simon," she told him angrily.

"Why?"

She glared at him, her face flushing a deep red.
"Because, I bet he knew. I would bet that he knew
who the heart was meant to go to. And I would
hazard a guess that he had told his wife. In fact, I
wouldn't be surprised if they had done it together!"

Mark frowned, backing away slightly. "But, why
would he put your name down as the one to get the
heart? I mean, you're not sick... are you?"

She sighed. "No. I'm not. But that is completely
besides the point."

"Perhaps they thought you were having an affair
with him then?"

She frowned. She'd never seen him, so that's not
likely. "I don't know this man."

He sighed, running his hands through his hair.
Racking his brain for any explanation he could
conjure up.

"Well... How many Claire Wittles do you think are
around here?" he gestured towards the station.
"Maybe one of them had the affair or something?"

She supposed that would make some sort of sense.
And with her being well known in the police force,
her name and photo would be the first to pop up on
local searches.

She lowered her head to the steering wheel, hoping the cool temperature of the plastic would ease the pounding she was feeling.

"Fine," she muttered. "And I would bet, that key would be to either a flat they rented together, or... maybe he bought her a house?"

"Why would he do that?" he frowned. "He was married, right?"

Claire tilted her head to one side. A thought popped into her head. "What if he had asked her for a divorce?"

"Asked who?"

"The wife. What if, before he died, he asked his wife for a divorce and she found out about the affair?"

He thought for a moment. "I dunno. It could be enough for her to rip his heart out herself, I suppose."

She climbed back out of the car, and headed for the closest office, rummaging through the drawers.

"What are you looking for?"

"The yellow pages. Grab one, we're gonna be there for a while."

"Ok. Then what?"

"Then," she said, getting fired up again. "We called divorce attorneys to find out which one he called. If he asked for a divorce, it'll be on record."

Mark smiled, and grabbed one from another desk.

"All right. Let's do this."

They sat at their desks, pounding out the numbers, ticking them off one by one.

After an hour of calling though, they finally got through to a lawyer, who seemed to be familiar with the name.

"What did you say this is for?" the lawyer asked again, for the dozenth time.

"To find out if Mr Stone filed for a divorce."

"Oh. For a case, right?"

"Yes," Claire replied. "His murder."

"Oh, ok. Well, yes, it does appear that he had filed for a divorce... six weeks ago."

Mark frowned, turning towards his partner. "Six weeks. So, that's more than enough time for the wife to know about the affair, right?"

Claire nodded. "Yeah, I reckon so." She paused, then spoke to the lawyer again. "Was the divorce papers signed?"

"No," he responded. "He's still waiting on it."

Claire turned to Mark again. "Still waiting? But he's served her the papers, right?"

The lawyer sighed. "I assume so. They've been separated for about eight weeks now."

Claire thanked him and hung up. She turned back to Mark. "She knows," she stated, pointing towards the door. "She played us."

Chapter Nine

They arrived back at George Rock's house about an hour later. Claire knocked on the door, smashing her knuckles against the polished wooden surface.

"H-Hello," a weak voice asked, from the other side of the door.

"Cut the act, *Sharon*, let us in. we need to talk."

The door opened, and the widow revealed herself, wearing a long red dress - nothing like the black gown she was wearing just days before."

"Going out?" Mark questioned.

"Yes. I-I'm meeting a friend."

Claire smirked. "Simon called, did he?"

Her face flushed a deep red.

"Yes, I imagine he called sometime last night."

Claire commented, "But, you've been seeing him a lot longer than Jimmy had been seeing Claire, haven't you."

"I don't know what you're talking about," she replied defensively. "He's just a friend."

"The same *friend* who had asked for your husband days before his death, who shut up like a clam when asked about him? *That* friend?"

She looked away, avoiding Claire's look of disdain.

"You sicken me," Claire told her, disgusted. "You knew about the affair, and you knew he asked you for a divorce. But you were simply holding back for when you killed him - then when he dies, you inherit."

"Yes," she hissed. "I knew about your sordid affair with my husband. But I didn't kill him, but believe me, I wish I had. I would have enjoyed it greatly!"

"First off, I did not have an affair with your husband. I'm too damn busy with my own life than to interfere with anyone else's. Secondly, I bet you were the one who planned his murder."

She glared back at her. "You think I did this? Prove it. You ain't got nothing on me, *homewrecker*."

"Homewrecker? Bitch, you'd been sleeping with Simon long before your husband started cheating."

"How dare you!" she shrieked. "I loved him!"

Claire shrugged, no longer treating the widow as the victim. "Sure you did. But you loved the money more."

Gotten what confirmation she needed, she left the house, scathing. She climbed back in her car, with her head pounding.

"What next?" Mark asked.

Claire looked forward, hardening her resolve. She had been too kind for too long. It was time to go back to her signature style, and kick their asses. "To get the proof she asked for. Let's see what the Captain had found out about that key."

The captain was hunched over her desk when they reached the office door. The frosted glass planes offered little vision, but they could see the blurry shape of her head and shoulders humped over in front of the computer.

"What do you mean you can't tell me?!" she screamed.

Claire shot Mark a concerned look, before thrusting open the door. They stood in the doorway, watching as the Captain's face glowed red. The lit lamp on her desk highlighted her high cheekbones, and hid her sunken eyes in shadow. At a glimpse, her face resembled a skull.

"What's wrong?" Mark asked, stepping forwards.

"What's wrong," she began, slamming down the phone, "is that the government won't tell me where the key opens. We're on our own."

Claire nodded. "That makes sense. We may have a lead though. The husband asked his wife for a divorce, but she didn't sign it. So, she either knew that he was going to die, or was waiting for the affair to come out and get a sympathetic vote for something."

"Have you been able to track down anyone who had an affair with him?"

Mark lowered his gaze, saying nothing. Claire shook her head. "Not yet. But my best guess, the key will certainly shine a light on that... as soon as we know where it goes..."

"And how do you suppose we do that?" she frowned, picking up the key from her desk. "It looks like any other key."

Claire pried the key from her fingers, holding it delicately as she frowned. She hoped, taking a closer look at it, it would reveal some sort of clue. That's when she saw it.

"Interesting," Claire mused.

"What?"

She held the key up and looked at them with a smile. "How many decorators are in the area?"

The captain frowned. "I don't know. Why?"

She smiled, feeling hopeful once more, letting the light of the lamp shine on the metal. In the grooves hidden on the side of the key's head, were flecks of blue chrome paint.

"What kind of decorator would use chrome paint for a house?" Claire frowned.

Mark smirked. "Oh, I can think of something."

He paused, smirking. They waited for him to continue.

Claire raised an eyebrow. "You gonna tell us or do we have to guess?"

"Oh, right. The only people that decorate with chrome paint are the ones who have a garage attached."

Claire smiled. "Of course. Cars. I can't see someone using chrome on just any model though, right?"

Mark shook his head. "No. Not just any model. It would be for people with really nice cars. Chrome paint isn't cheap either, so we're looking for someone with money."

Claire frowned. "Well, that narrows it down to a few houses, half the houses down here have garages. And with cars like that, it won't be left in an open garage. It'd be put away."

Mark grinned. "You should check out my page more. There's a car meet once a month. I can bet that someone down there will match the paint, and know where to get the paint from."

"Better, the killer might be at the meet."

They looked at each other, their eyes met. They fell silent, as their faces looked at one another.

"Don't just stand there," the captain said, speaking up. "Go get something to eat, and then get on with it. Find out the location of the next meet up."

Mark scrolled through his phone, glancing at the images of super cars and new body wraps the drivers had bought. A few members of the facebook page shared pictures and videos of before and after reactions, behind the scenes, and even the process of custom made attachments.

Claire shook her head, only guessing at the expense they must have spent on them. She knew, from repairs on her cars over the years, the basic needs of the car parts were hundreds of pounds. She shuddered to think of what the price tag would be for a wrap, though she had heard that it could run well into the thousands.

She frowned again, putting the key back on to the desk. She paused, tapping her fingers together, cringing. Then wiped her fingers along her coat. The captain frowned.

"What's wrong?" she asked.

"Nothing," Claire replied, not wanting to be rude. "My hands were a little sticky from the key, but it's fine."

The captain stared at her for a moment. "Yeah, the key seemed sticky to me, too."

Mark held out his hand, reaching for the key. "What kind of sticky?"

"What kind?" Claire repeated, baffled. "It's sticky. So, the sticky kind."

"No. There's different types of sticky. Like sticky from adhesive, or sticky like glue transfer..."

"I dunno. It's just sticky," she told him, scowling. Mark reached out an open palm. Sighing, Claire passed him the key.

"There, have at it."

He grimaced. "Yeah, that's sticky all right. Tacky sticky."

"Tack--What are you talking about?"

"Tacky. You know, like the type of sticky when something had been spilled and not cleaned up properly, and it leaves the surface kinda sticky."

She blinked. "I wouldn't know. I don't clean up without bleach."
He laughed. "Well, I have. You've clearly never spilled beer on a night out or had to clean up after a house party."

Claire frowned. The thought of having people in her house, making a mess of her home repulsed her.
"Why would your friends disrespect your home like that?" she asked. "If I have people around, then they should clear up spillages."
Mark l;aughed and shook his head. "This is why you're not invited to parties. You're too uptight."
She glared at him in silent retort. He smirked and returned his attention to the captain. "The key was next to whatever was spilled."
"And?"
"Well, with the surface being sticky, we might be able to get a fingerprint from it."
Claire looked hopeful for a moment, and turned towards him.
"You think so? There's a problem with that."
"Why?"
She raised an eyebrow. "Because we have all handled it. If there were prints on the key, it would not be completely unusable. We have all touched the key, without gloves - hence the sticky."
His face fell crestfallen. "Oh yeah," he said deflated. "I hadn't thought of that."

"Don't beat yourself up," she told him. She turned towards the captain. "It does make me think though..." she said, facing them both. "If his or her hands were sticky, maybe the fingerprint was transferred to something else as well as the key."

"Like the box it came in!" Mark gasped.

Claire nodded. She rushed back to her desk and grabbed the small box carefully, trying not to touch it.

"We still touched the box," he said, chasing after her.

"Perhaps, but the box would be a lot less contaminated than the key - so hopefully it'd be usable."

She put the box in an envelope and labelled it, then sent it to the lab.

"Ok," she sighed, smiling. "While we wait for that, we'll go and find the Claire he had been having an affair with."

Chapter Ten

After calling several names in the local area, all with the name of Claire Wittle, she hung up the phone. She ticked them off the list, one by one to no avail. Then, reaching the last one at the bottom of the page, she dialled, keeping her fingers crossed.

"Hello?" a woman answered.

"Hello. Is this Claire Wittle?"

"It is. Who's calling?"

"Uh. I'm Detective Wittle of the Wardgar Homicide department."

"Oh? How can I help you?"

"Well, I'm wondering if you've heard of George Rocks, or Jimmy Stone?"

She paused, waiting.

"No. I've not heard of them. Who are they?"

"I can't say much, it's an ongoing investigation. But we're lead to believe a victim had an affair with a Claire Wittle."

"I see. I'm sorry I couldn't help. I don't have a boyfriend, and I have no interest in having one." She paused, wondering if she should say more. "I... I don't like boys like that."

"That's fine. Thank you for your time."

Claire hung up and crossed the name off the list.

"That was the last one. If the husband is having an affair with a woman called Claire, then it's not someone on the yellow pages. They either don't exist and gave him a false name, or she only has a cell phone."

Mark frowned, his demeanour starting to sour. "What now?"

That was a good question. "Well," she said, thinking as she spoke, "I think we should check the cameras again. Perhaps we can get a face from the CCTV cameras, or shop cameras in the area. Someone has seen something."

Claire hated the idea of having to go back to door-to-door knocking but she was left with few options.

"Hi," she said, greeting the first woman to answer the door across the street.

"Yes?"

"Hi. I was just wondering if you'd seen someone hanging about lately?"

She frowned, ruffling her long silvery-grey hair.

"No. I've not seen anyone. Sorry."

"Did you hear anything?" Claire prompted.

Again the woman shook her head. "No. Sorry."

Each house she knocked pretty much had the same answers.

Claire glanced towards Mark, who didn't seem to be having better luck.

By the time they reached the end of the road, they'd run out of doors and people to question. It all seemed like the case was getting cooler by the minute.

"What now?"

Claire sighed. She wished she knew.

"I think we'll need to go back to my original suspects, since we know they're right in the middle of it. The widow seems to be having an affair of her own, and I don't know how Simon is involved, he might just be feeding her information. But that doesn't explain or tell us about how or why the heart ended up on my desk. Just the motive to kill him. And to have him as the donor after all, muddies the water somewhat."

"I agree," Mark replied. He glanced down at the time.

"It's getting late. How about I buy you dinner and then we try again in the morning."

Claire smiled, and tucked a strand behind her ear. "All right. Pick me up at Nine, so I can change into some fresh clothes."

He laughed lightly but agreed. "I'll see you soon."

When Claire arrived home, she had her shower and changed into a long black dress, the type of dress that has discrete pockets on the sides. It was her favourite feature. She didn't use it, it wasn't deep enough for much. So, she dug out a small handbag from her wardrobe, then dropped her phone and keys into the bag's pocket. She smiled, catching a glimpse of her reflection in the mirror.

She pulled a brush through her hair, then tied it into a ponytail, then gave a final layer of lipstick to her makeup. She smiled again, looking forward to the night ahead.

The doorbell rang the moment it turned nine.

She swung open the door on the first chime.
"Wow," he gasped. Mark was wearing a suit, with a deep red tie.
His hair was slicked back with gel, and she could smell the familiar scent of his cologne he was wearing. She thought back to the shirt he let her wear. It was in the wash, now.

She smiled back at him, tucking a strand of hair behind her ear.
"Thank you," she said, smoothing down her dress. "I thought this one would suit me better."

They arrived at the restaurant and were led to a table at the far end of the room, closer to the kitchen. Claire inhaled deeply, taking in the aroma of the roast chicken filling the room. Her mouth watered.
"You know..." Mark said, pulling up a chair. "If he had mentioned your name a lot, maybe the key makers would be able to answer where the key goes to, if you ask?"
"What do you mean?" Claire frowned.
"Just saying. If they all think you're having an affair with the man, maybe he gave them permission to tell you stuff that others aren't allowed to know. Private stuff."
She sighed, thinking about it. "Perhaps. But if the other Claire Wittle turns up, what then?"

He shrugged. "Then she can take it up with you, since it was your desk his heart was left on."

As much as she hated to admit it, she was running out of options.

"All right," she sighed, defeated. "In the morning, we'll see what they say. Maybe they'll tell us. Maybe they won't. And we can ask if they have seen him recently at the same time. Also, get his phone records. I have a feeling we might find something there too."

Claire had no idea what she was going to do next, at this point she was just winging it. She frowned, struggling to think of what her next move could possibly be. That's when she remembered. "We need to see who else had motive for wanting him dead. But for the women's partners he was nice to, where would we find them?"

"At their houses probably," Mark replied.

She nodded, and watched as the waitress approached them holding the menus.

"Here are the menus. Today's specials are cod curry with cauliflower and potatoes. There is also vegetable risotto, for a vegetarian and vegan friendly meal."

"Wonderful," she said smiling. It was a hard choice, but she wasn't interested in having a heavy meal. At least, not for that evening.

"I don't know about you, but I think I'll have the fish curry."

Mark nodded. "Sounds good."

The waitress nodded, writing down the orders. "What about drinks?"

Mark didn't hesitate. "I'll have an americano coffee."

Claire thought for a moment. "Hmm. Coffee sounds great, but which one?" She glanced down at the options. Cappuccino, americano, latte, mocha... all her favourite options. She sighed, and settled for her usual. "I'll have the latte please."

The waitress thanked them, and then carried the orders to the kitchen. Claire hoped it wouldn't take too long to cook.

"As I was saying," Claire commented, continuing her train of thought. "If we go to the houses, it's going to take a while – what if they go to work?"

"Good point," he mused. He thought for a moment. "What about we go down to the block where he was incarcerated. If he had time, he would have been able to do some talking."

Did he do time? She couldn't remember. Claire went back to the computer, double checking, and to find out which facility Jimmy Stones had done time in. He hadn't. She groaned. "Well, that's a no-go." She shook her head. Time for another plan. She looked at the information she had on him, and thought out loud. "We still need to find out where the key goes."

"Wait – have we finished checking all the Claire Wittle names? We had that one who said it sounded familiar, right?"

"Oh yeah!" she gasped. She grabbed her notes; surprised that she had forgotten she had taken them, and then made her way down to the paragraph of where the woman lived. "Let's pay her a visit," Claire stated. "If she knows him, great. If not, then we'll need another way to find out where the key goes to."

"if she doesn't know, it may be worth asking the state yourself – especially if you're on his will. You are in his will to inherit his heart after all."

He had a point. "all right," she agreed.

Chapter Eleven

The journey to Claire Wittle's apartment was almost half an hour's journey.

The detective was curious to see how the other version of her lived. Was she a wealthy woman? Was she living on the breadline? Did she have children? Was she married?" she frowned. If she was married and had an affair with Jimmy, that would make her less of an honourable woman – and would certainly give her name... well, a bad name. She shook her head, telling herself that the woman's behaviour was no reflection on her. Not that she believed it, but she told herself anyway.

They pulled up to a small apartment block that was located between a bakery and a pizza house. Not a bad location, but she would have been sick of the smell of pizza after a while. She grimaced, but climbed out of the car and approached the front door. The number nineteen was nailed to the door, and painted on the wall beside it. She took a deep breath and knocked.

"Hello?" a woman's voice called out.

"Hi. I'm detective Wittle, we spoke on the phone yesterday."

The door opened, revealing a middle-aged woman wearing a blue dress and had auburn hair. She had dark red lipstick and three shades of yellow eyeshadow on.

"You didn't have to come down here," she said, greeting them at the door.
"I kind of did," the detective replied, taking out her notebook.
She riffled through the pages, and pulled out a photograph of the picture of the victim. The self portrait found on his social media page, rather than the image of how he was found.
"Do you recognise him at all?"
She took the photo, and studied his face carefully.
"No. I'm sorry. I must have just heard the name over the news or something. I'm sorry you wasted your time."
The woman closed the door, leaving the detective and her partner standing on the porch, still holding the photograph.

"Well. That didn't go the way I expected it to."
Claire agreed. "She was the last one on the list. So, he wasn't having an affair. There must be another reason why someone took his heart, and why he had signed his heart to another woman."

"It also means, it is possible that it was meant for you. Do you know him, maybe you have seen him around at a glance?" Mark asked.

Claire wished she had answers, but now they were no closer than they were at the beginning. "I hate this case," she muttered, shaking her head. "If only there was a way to find out where that key goes to."

"I told you," Mark insisted. "Ask the state. If my theory is right, he's put your name on more than one item."

As much as she hated the thought, she couldn't see any other alternative. "All right," she sighed, defeatedly. "I'll give them a call. But the sooner we solve this damn case, the better."

Claire had no idea what she was going to do next, at this point she was just winging it. She frowned, struggling to think of what her next move could possibly be. That's when she remembered. "We need to see who else had motive for wanting him dead. But for the women's partners he was nice to, where would we find them?"

"At their houses probably," Mark replied.

She nodded, and watched as the waitress approached them holding the menus.

"Here are the menus. Today's specials are cod curry with cauliflower and potatoes. There is also vegetable risotto, for a vegetarian and vegan friendly meal."

"Wonderful," she said smiling. It was a hard choice, but she wasn't interested in having a heavy meal. At least, not for that evening.

"I don't know about you, but I think I'll have the fish curry."

Mark nodded. "Sounds good."

The waitress nodded, writing down the orders. "What about drinks?"

Mark didn't hesitate. "I'll have americano coffee."

Claire thought for a moment. "Hmm. Coffee sounds great, but which one?" She glanced down at the options. Cappuccino, americano, latte, mocha... all her favourite options. She sighed, and settled for her usual. "I'll have the latte please."

The waitress thanked them, and then carried the orders to the kitchen. Claire hoped it wouldn't take too long to cook.

"As I was saying," Claire commented, continuing her train of thought. "If we go to the houses, it's going to take a while – what if they go to work?"

"Good point," he mused. He thought for a moment. "What about we go down to the block where he was incarcerated. If he had time, he would have been able to do some talking."

Did he do time? She couldn't remember. Claire went back to the computer, double checking, and to find out which facility Jimmy Stones had done time in. He hadn't. She groaned. "Well, that's a no-go." She shook her head. Time for another plan. She looked at the information she had on him, and thought out loud. "We still need to find out where the key goes."

"Wait! Have we finished checking all the Claire wittle names? We had that one who said it sounded familiar, right?"

"Oh yeah!" she gasped. She grabbed her notes; surprised that she had forgotten she had taken them, and then made her way down to the paragraph of where the woman lived. "Let's pay her a visit," Claire stated. "If she knows him, great. If not, then we'll need another way to find out where the key goes to."

"if she doesn't know, it may be worth asking the state yourself – especially if you're on his will. You are on his will to inherit his heart after all."

He had a point. "all right," she agreed.

The journey to Claire Wittle's apartment was almost an hour.

The detective was curious to see how the other version of her lived. Was she a wealthy woman? Was she living on the breadline? Did she have children? Was she married?" she frowned. If she was married and had the affair with Jimmy, that would make her less of an honourable woman – and would certainly give her name... well, a bad name. She shook her head, telling herself that the woman's behaviour was no reflection on her. Not that she believed it, but she told herself anyway.

They pulled up to a small apartment block that was located between a bakery and a pizza house. Not a bad location, but she would have been sick of the smell of pizza after a while. She grimaced, but climbed out of the car and approached the front door. The number nineteen was nailed to the door, and painted on the wall beside it. She took a deep breath and knocked.

"Hello?" a woman's voice called out.

"Hi. I'm detective Wittle, we spoke on the phone yesterday."

The door opened, revealing a middle-aged woman wearing a blue dress and had auburn hair. She had dark red lipstick and three shades of yellow eyeshadow on.

Taking the advice from her partner, Claire drove down to the state building with the key in hand. She was sure they would tell her nothing, but it wouldn't be from lack of trying; especially when she was running out of ideas.

The building towered above them. The white granite glistened in the light, speckled with the occasional grey pebble, embedded in the walls.

Claire took a deep breath and went inside, listening to the sounds of people talking in hushed tones and her heels tapping against the floor. She strode over to the front desk, straightening her posture. She had no idea how she was going to broach the subject, and was half expecting to be told to "do one" or something of that nature.

The receptionist was a redhead with glasses. She was wearing a navy blue jacket over a white shirt, looking somewhat serious.

"Hello…" she leaned in, glancing at the name tag on the front of the jacket. "…Janet. I'm wondering if you can help us. I was sent this key, but I need to know what it opens."

The woman sighed, then looked up. Noting Claire and Mark's uniform, she cleared her throat and held out an open hand.

"Let me take a look for you," she said, faking a smile. Claire passed her the key, and watched as the woman studied the size of the key and inspected the jagged edges along its length.

"It's a door key," she stated simply.

Claire rolled her eyes. "No kidding. Can you find the door it opens for me? Please?"

She frowned, narrowing her eyes. "What did you say your name was?"

"Detective Claire Wittle," she replied.

"Oh ok. Let me just check the system."

She tapped a few buttons on the keyboard and then nodded. "Yes, here it is."

Claire waited patiently, for Janet to give her the information. After a few moments of silence, Claire prompted her again. "Well?"

"I'm gonna need to see your ID."

Claire sighed again, not understanding why she hadn't asked for that in the first place. She took out her id, and her police badge. "Better?"

Janet nodded, looking a little flustered. "It's to a storage room door. Unit 23A, block 3... Hanzel Road." she paused before continuing. "Do you need the postcode?"

"Yes please," Claire replied.

"Don't bother," Mark stated. "I know where that is."

Claire frowned and looked at him. "You do?"

He nodded. "I had a few cases in the area a couple years ago. People using the units to house their black market products."

"Ooh," she breathed. "All right then. Well, let's go and find out what Jimmy had been hiding."

She let Mark take the wheel, since he knew where to go. She had no idea. Smiling, she took the precious few minutes to relax and watch the world pass her by. The roads and pavements were cracked, like a long branch stretching out as far as it could reach, splitting into smaller branches along the way. Webbed pavement stones framed the crossroads, and the trees divided on both sides, full of pink and white blossoms filled the streets with colour against the backdrop of green uneven grass and the bright blue sky. Spring was definitely making itself known, with the promise of warmer weather to come, and she couldn't wait.

Hanzel Road was pretty much what she expected. The structure was grey, the flooring was uneven, holy and cracked. The unit doors were painted blue and yellow, and each block was divided between odd and even numbers.

She couldn't help but notice a small group of children. She pointed towards them. "What do you think they're up to?" He looked to where she was pointing and frowned.

"Stay here," he said, telling her firmly. "I'll go and get them to clear out. We don't know what'll come out of those doors, and we don't want them getting hurt."

"Good idea," she said, nodding. "This is no place for children."

Kate watched as he made his way over to the group, flashing his badge on his belt. She frowned, watching them step back warily, before running off in the opposite direction in a hurry.

When he returned, he opened the door with a satisfied smile. "I warned them this place was dangerous and sent them home, or to hang about somewhere safer. I don't think they have homes to go to. They had some bedding behind the bushes by the building."

"Oh ok..." she felt bad but nodded. "Let's get this over with."

Mark pointed towards the far end, where she could just about make out the fading label of the 23A on the door. She passed Mark the key, and watched as he slipped the key into the lock and turned it. The door opened with a click.

Chapter Twelve

They walked into the storage unit with questions still whirling inside her head. Even if the storage room gave away the killer's identity, how did he (or she) slip a package onto her desk without anyone seeing or noticing? There were still so many questions left unanswered.
Claire followed Mark into the room. He was quiet, and his back was surprisingly rigid. He strode across the room and seemingly found the light switch with ease. She frowned, watching as the room lit up.
The storage room was nothing she was expecting. Rather than a dank, cluttered space filled with boxes

and papers, she was met instead with what appeared to be a wall, covered with a sheet of lace curtain.

"What's this?" she questioned herself, inching towards the large covered area. The curtain glistened, revealing the speckled glitter scattered across the light pink fabric.

"A shrine, I guess," Mark replied, though not in his usual quizzical tone.

Something was definitely off with him, she was sure of it.

"What's the matter?" she asked him, looking at him with concern.

"It's nothing," he muttered, his tone hardened; warning her not to press. She sighed and gave him a defeated nod.

As she looked around, she was surprised to see that the wall was filled with photographs. Some were printed as a landscape image, others were upright. A few, she noted, looked like they had been cut out from newspapers. She stepped closer to the featured wall, heading towards the veil when a chill ran down her spine.

"They're me!" she gasped, feeling nauseous. "All of the photos are of me!" Her stomach turned, and she reached out to the vail before grabbing a large handful of the lacy fabric, then yanked hard, ripping the cover off the wall. Mark was right. Behind the fabric, a table stood in an alcove. On the table, three candles were half-melted, and between them was a large portrait of Claire. She peered closer to the image, recognising a green lampshade in the background, perched on a small circular table. Her flesh turned cold, and her heart skipped a beat. The photograph was taken from outside her home.

Claire looked around in shock and disbelief as the gut-wrenching realisation hit her. The killer had been spying on her. Her head spun, struggling to grasp what she was seeing. Grabbing hold of the wall, her only thought that made sense was the killer was either a neighbour or a friend.

She didn't like those options. "This just doesn't make sense," she stated, scratching her head. "Who would take pictures of me like this?" She also didn't remember having her picture done. "This is recent, in the last six months," she said, turning to Mark. "I bought that lamp after christmas. Some of these images are even older..."

She walked the length of the decorated wall, looking for anything that could be a clue. All of the photos were taken at a distance, and most of them were taken outside or through a window. She paused, and grabbed a pair of latex gloves from her pocket, pulling them on. "There's one advantage of having pictures taken through glass," she said with a smile. "What's that?" Mark asked. He watched her pull a handful of images from the wall. She frowned, looking back at him over her shoulder.

"Reflections," she replied with a smirk. "Grab all the photos shot through glass. I'm certain, the killer's face will come up in at least one of these, and I'm going to find it."

The drive back to the station was done in silence. Claire flipped through the photographs at a glance. "Twenty," she counted irritably. "Twenty pictures. Photos, shrines, a heart..." she listed. She couldn't keep the desperation from her voice. "Why me? I'm nothing special. I'm plain, boring, and let's be honest, I'm not exactly a model!"

"Stop it," Mark muttered, glaring at her. "You're beautiful. At least you're noticed. Not like me," he told her sternly. "I'm invisible."

Claire laughed hard.

"What?" he demanded, snapping his head round to face her.

"I don't know what's funnier," she replied, still laughing in fits. "That you think you're unnoticed, or that you're invisible!"

"Why is that funny?"

"Because," she told him in a matter of fact tone. "I have always noticed you. If this case had not landed on my desk, you wouldn't have known I existed. You wouldn't have looked at me twice. I was invisible to everyone. You, you have the attention of every woman in the precinct. You are the most visible, and noticed man I have ever known."

He frowned, looking at her for a long moment. "You noticed me?"

"Yes! I noticed!" she laughed, then turned, blushing. "I noticed when you changed your tie after last week's lunch break. I noticed when you cut your hair. I noticed when you lean over the tables, and always rest your right elbow up against the wall when you're talking about backstreets."

His expression shifted, from uncertainty to vacant. His demeanour shifted too, as he stood leaning slightly to the left. His eyes flitted around the room, searching his mind.

"You always liked me?"

The corner of her mouth twitched. "Yeah. But you wouldn't have noticed. You paid more attention to Valerie."

"Valerie?" he repeated. "The receptionist?"

She nodded, then watched as he laughed.

"Valerie is not my type. And she's dating my sister."

Claire blinked, feeling foolish. "Oh. Well..." she cleared her throat and peered back down at the photos. "Either way," she said, getting back on topic. "I'm gonna know who the killer is. One of these pictures are gonna have his reflection on it. I just need to find the right one."

The journey back seemed to take a lot longer than the way there. She glared at the image, scolding it into revealing who the killer was. Something niggled at her, though, she wasn't sure what. Something seemed... off.

"You seem quite. Is everything alright?" Mark asked, looking at her with a side-eyed glance.

"Oh? Yeah, yeah. I'm fine," she replied, not in the mood to indulge. The thoughts of the storage room occupied her, revisiting what she saw. A shrine. A shudder shook her body.

"Are you sure?" he asked her.

"Yes..."

He fell silent and turned his attention to the window, watching as the old abandoned houses of the lower end of the town passed them by. Boarded up windows covered in spray paint, and doors that should've been closed, hung on their hinges, neglected for many years. Houses, she noted, should have been either repaired or demolished a long time ago.

Finally, they arrived back at the station. The carpark was full, as per usual, leaving them with no other option but to park at the very back of the parking lot. She sighed, her day was not getting any better.

"What did you find out?" the captain asked, without skipping a beat.

He stood in the doorway just as Kate and Mark entered the room.

He was wearing a suit with a tie, that seemed a lot smarter than his usual attire.

"It was strange," she told him. "There was a shrine with a lot of pictures of me in it. And, one of the pictures looked inside this very room. So, there's either a secret camera, or someone has been looking through the window... I think I can catch the reflection in the image though."

"Interesting. Let me know how it goes," he told her, puffing out his chest.

"Sir, you're looking... formal. What's the occasion?"

"I'm going on a date," he replied casually. "Go on home, you can take care of the photograph in the morning."

Kate smiled. "I hope you have a good time," she said, not waiting around for him to change his mind. She shoved the photos into the evidence box, save one, and closed it tight. The faster she identifies the killer, the faster she can have her wine.

The apartment was in complete darkness by the time she arrived home. She flicked the switch, sighing. Nothing. She rolled her eyes, flicking it again, as if she expected the reverse. She tried again. The darkness remained. Huffing impatiently, she stumbled her way through to the living room to attempt at the next light. That one didn't light up either. Two bulbs not working? Not likely. She took out her phone and used the torch to find her way to the fuse box. Nothing wrong there. "Great," she muttered indignantly to herself. "The electricity is out, again." That would be the second time that month. With nothing else to offer her to lighten up the black void of her home, she took out a candle from her kitchen draw and lit it. Then, she screamed.

Chapter Thirteen

The scene in front of her was worse than she had ever seen in her life. The living room was completely trashed. Drawers were strewn across the room, cupboards had been emptied over the floor,and the windows were broken. The sofa, too, had been torn apart. Was this meant to be a message, or were they looking for something? Fear clutched her throat, as she wondered if the intruder was still inside her house. She pulled out her gun from its holster, and held it out in front of her. She steadied her staggered breathing, trying to get her heart to stop beating outside her chest.
She walked through the broken glass that cracked beneath her feet. She held her breath around every corner until she made her way into the kitchen. There, nothing was touched, except for a note pinned to the fridge door. One written in her hand, a reminder to buy some more milk. She scanned the

kitchen with a frown and discovered the reminder scrunched up and laying on the floor next to the waste basket. "What the hell is going on?"she muttered to herself. Her eyes darted towards the stairs to the bedroom. She swallowed hard, then carefully made her way up each step, being careful not to tread on the squeaky slab half way up.
The door to her bedroom was open. In the gap between the door and it's frame, she could just about make out the bedding laying on the floor in a heap. The window of that room, also wide open. Something she hadn't done in several months, due to the flies and spider nests in the ivy nearby. She licked her dry lips, holding her gun steady.
Ready to fight, she burst into the room. Empty. She considered replacing the gun back into its holder, but decided to give the apartment a final check before being satisfied that she was alone. Then, she decided, she would have no option but to call it in - despite having to tread through the evidence laying across her floor.

Satisfied that she was in no immediate danger, she took out her phone and called it in. She muttered to herself, opening the fridge door. Still no milk, but she knew that anyway. She glanced at the bottle of wine. "Well, at least that was still untouched," she sighed. She pulled out a magnifying glass app on her iphone, checking that the seal had been untouched.

Thankfully, no holes were visible. She turned towards her kitchen units and made herself a fresh mug of coffee and slipped a cap full of some martini liquor into her coffee. It wasn't quite the kick she was looking for, but it was enough to take the edge off her nerves.

She had just managed to drink half a cup before there was a knock on the door. She carried the cup with her as she made her way to the front door. Mark was standing in the doorway, holding out his gun. His eyes narrowed, scanning her. "Are you all right? Are you hurt?"

She shook her head. "No. I am just shaken. Whoever it was has made a mess of... everything. Other than the kitchen. I don't know if they were looking for something, or trying to warn me off... I just don't know."

"It could just be someone who is trying to scare you off..." he agreed, looking around at her in the mess. "Can I come in?"

She nodded and stepped aside, watching as he walked through the hallway. Then, in the living room he stopped at the door, gasping.

"I know," she said, shaking her head. "Trust me. I know. They trashed the stairs as well. The only places that hadn't been obliterated were the kitchen and the bathroom. But, I don't know who would do this."

"It had to be someone who knew where you live," he told her.

Kate sighed. That was obvious. Then again, it could have been a random hit, and someone hoped to be able to find something worth stealing.

"Is anything missing?" he asked.

She shook her head. "I don't know. I don't want to touch more things - I've already contaminated the broken glass on the floor by walking over it when I checked the house."

"You didn't call it in immediately?" he sounded almost cross.

"No. I wanted to make sure I was in no immediate danger before I did anything else. Also, I didn't want to scare off anyone that might have been left behind. So no, I didn't immediately call it in."

He rolled his eyes and sat down. "Sorry, it has been a long day."

"No fucking kidding," she retorted.

A shadowed figure walked in, standing in the living room doorway. "Damn," he said. Kate blinked, almost spilling her coffee. "You didn't close the door behind yourself?" she gasped.

He laughed. "No, I knew you'd have company. Got the forensics on the way, and the captain wanted to make sure you were all right."

She sighed, reluctantly slumping her shoulders. "I- I just don't know if someone is going to come back. What if this was a trap?"

"If this was a trap, then the intruder would have been back already. Have you noticed anything missing?"

Again, she shook her head. "Maybe I should check." She made her way up to the bedroom where her drawers were emptied. Everything was emptied over the now-bare mattress. The clothes were pulled off every hanger and toppled out of every drawer. She reached under her bed and pulled out a small box. It was unlocked, and empty.

"Shit," she muttered. Tears stung her eyes.

"Something is missing," she said, holding out her box to the others.

"What was in it?" the captain asked.

He took off his coat, revealing the suit he was still wearing. She gasped, in all the chaos, she had forgotten that he was meant to be on a date. She groaned. "Oh, I am so sorry," she cried out. "Your date!"

"It's fine," he consoled her. "It has been rearranged to be in a couple of days. Tell us what was in the box."

She swallowed a lump that got caught in her throat. "It was a diamond necklace... It was from my mother before she died. It was all I had left of her..."

Their face fell. "Kate... I am so sorry. Look, we'll do what we can to find it. Ok?"

As much as she appreciated the thought, she knew as well as they did that the chances of ever seeing it again, was slim to none. She nodded anyway, and turned her attention to the fridge. "Why did they rip off my reminder?" she frowned. It simply didn't make sense.

"What are you talking about?"

Kate pointed to the fridge in the kitchen. "I had a note to remind myself to get some more milk. I hadn't got it yet. But, I found it scrunched up on the floor. Why leave the rest of the kitchen but take down my note?"

Their faces looked just as confused as hers. She made her way into the kitchen to where she saw it last and picked it up from the floor. Carefully, trying not to touch too much of the paper, she unfolded the paper and spread it out across the table. The word milk had been scribbled out with a red pen. In its place was a word written in all caps. "Don't forget to..." she skipped past the scribbled words that was meant to be "buy milk" and instead read the words scribbled beside it. "Die." She blinked, reading it again. "Don't forget to die..."

It definitely wasn't a random robbery. Someone knew where she lived and had made sure she knew it. This wasn't someone warning her off a case. This was a different message altogether, a message that someone was coming after her and that her days were numbered.

"Right, you clearly can't stay here tonight," the captain announced with a stern tone. "You'll be staying at one of the safehouse until we know what is going on."

"Safe house?" she objected. "How can I solve the case of the heartless valentine if you're sending me away to hide?"

"Mark will have to team up with someone else. You're in too much danger."

"What about him?" she argued. "Was there anyone there? Is your place next?" she asked Mark, turning to him in desperation.

"No," he replied. "Nothing."

She shook her head. Her stomach was making noises and she felt sick. When was the last time she ate? She sighed, listening to him list his concerns. "First the heart, then the shrine and the photographs, and now this. You are clearly the target," he said. The captain agreed. "Until this is solved, you'll be staying at the hotel in the east - the one by the ocean. Only us will be the ones to know the location. If anyone else asks, we'll tell them that you're staying with family."

She went to argue again, but was met with an angry glare and quickly shut her mouth again.

Chapter Fourteen

Kate sighed. "Fine. But I am not going anywhere without my coffee machine," she told them. The captain laughed but agreed, having seen what she was like without coffee, he decided that the better option was simply to agree. At least it wasn't a device that could have tracked her to the safehouse. "All right," he said. He pulled the plug, and helped her pack up the coffee and the accessories to go along with it, and one of her favourite mugs. When they were done, they led her back to one of the cars, ready for the long drive east to where they were going to hide her away. She took out the memory card from her phone and grabbed her old digital camera, and laptop. If she was going to be hiding, the least she could do is work.

When she arrived at the hotel, the sun was rising over the horizon, reflecting the warm orange glow across the watery surface. The water glistened gold, in the ripples of the water.

"You'll stay here," the captain told her. Kate nodded numbly, her eyes red and swollen from tiredness. The shadows beneath her eyes made her appear aged several years, that no amount of sleep could save. She cleared her throat before thanking him. The captain paused, thinking for a moment before turning over to Mark. "Listen, guard the door, will you?" he asked.

Mark frowned, looking taken aback for a moment. He straightened his posture and stuck out his chin defiantly. "Why?"

The captain raised his eyebrow and replied with slow deliberation. "Because I have asked you to. I don't know if we were followed, so stand here and guard the door, so that no one else knows where she is staying. Understood?"

Mark backed down and nodded, turning his attention to the door with a mutter. "Yes sir," he grumbled. "Whatever you say."

The captain lead Kate up the stairs, as she counted the floors on the way up. She stopped on the second from the last floor and walked through a door that was secured with a large metal bolt.

"You'll be staying here," he repeated.

"It's a long way up," she complained. "What if I need to escape?"

"You won't need to," he told her confidently. Then paused. "If you have to make a quick exit, there is a hidden door under the mat in the bathroom. It's a built in slide, and it will take you directly to the carpark cupboard - disguised as a janitor closet. There's a false wall behind it. But, you just need to push a button and it will swing open. All right?"

Feeling a little more at ease, she nodded and gestured to the other doors. "Which one is it?" she asked.

He smiled, and shrugged. "They all have it. I'm going to leave and you'll pick when I am out of sight. Understood. I'm not stupid. This way, Mark or I, will know which one you are in. Pick any of the next couple of floors. All of the rooms in the top three floors have the same exit. So, you'll be safe either way."

Kate hugged him, before stepping away awkwardly. "Thank you."

He nodded and walked out of the doors back towards the stairs. As soon as he was out of sight, she headed over to the door on the very end. Now, she just only hoped that she could use a private internet connection to make sure that she could solve the case before anyone finds her.

Taking off her coat, she pulled out the photograph from her inside pocket. The image was too distorted to see who was in the reflection to look with the naked eye. She would have to scan the photo itself into the computer and do some playing with the photo manipulator.

She used her digital camera and took a photograph of the image in front of her, and then plugged the memory stick from the camera into her computer, then, holding her breath, she uploaded the file.

She knew that it would take some time. Sighing, she plugged in the coffee machine and prepared herself a mug of coffee. There would be no sleeping tonight, she knew that much. Time was running against her, and even if no one else knew where she was, she was confident that whoever trashed her house would stop at nothing to find her. The question was, why?

And why was Mark behaving so strangely at the storage unit? What was he hiding?

She poured her cup of coffee and allowed her thoughts to stray. Mark had got to her house pretty fast. Yet, he hadn't broken a sweat. How fast did he drive to get to her? She smiled, it had been a long time since anyone had really worried about her in that way, or cared enough to turn up to check on her. She felt bad that she couldn't tell him where she was staying, but who knows what someone would do to him to find out her location. Some crazy person, leaving her a heart to find. Who's heart was it? A donor with a changed name, under witness protection - what good it did him. Poisoned perhaps? Would that come up? She took out her burner phone that came with the standard safehouse, and called the coroner.

"Hey Liz," she said, greeting her as if nothing had happened.

"Hey, Kate. Where are you calling from? I don't recognise this number?"

She brushed it off with the same excuse she gave guys. "I borrowed a phone from a friend, my one isn't working."

"Oh ok. What can I do for you?"

"Odd question," she told her. "I'm wondering if you can do an autopsy on the heart?"

"I already did that, remember? It was split in two with a knife."

She hadn't forgotten. She shuddered. "Yeah, I'm thinking it needs something else. Perhaps a toxin works?"

"Why?" Liz asked, curiosity creeping into her tone.

"Because, I want to know if there was any other reason why the heart would be donated to me - or whether the killer donated the heart to me, rather than the victim."

"Oh! That I can help you with!" she cheered. "The records. I dug into them after you left. The victim's handwriting doesn't match the ones his family provided. Which means the killer donated the heart to you, not the victim." She fell silent for a moment before continuing. "The handwriting looks really familiar... I'm going to have to check my files to see what other forgery cases we've had over the years. I know I have seen that handwriting before. I just can't place it..."

Kate shuddered again. "What possible reason would the killer have to send me the heart, and donate it to me? What happened to just handing me a valentine's card, or buying me a bottle of wine like normal people?"

"I know. Guys are stupid. Speaking of which, have you spoken to Mark yet?"

She paused. "Why?"

Liz cleared her throat. "He hasn't been in all day."

There was a reason for that, she knew. "Yeah, it's been a busy day. My house was broken into, so I have had to go and stay with family. So, you know, working from home. It sucks."

"I get that. Do you know who it was? What was stolen?"

Tears stung her eyes once again. "The necklace my mum gave me before she died. It was meant to be in a small box under the bed, but when I found it, it was unlocked and missing. And my house was completely destroyed."

The phone fell silent. "Are you still there?"

The sound of the dial tone blared from the speaker. She was disconnected. She rolled her eyes, and looked at the bars on her screen. What reception she had, was now gone. "Shit," she cussed. "Now what?"

She turned her attention to the computer screen, and waited for the image to finish loading up. It was almost done. After the last of the pixels appeared, she breathed a sigh of relief. Now she had something else to do whilst waiting around. She saved the image and then slowly, she zoomed in. Slowly, a familiar face came into view.

"No!" she gasped. Nausea swept over her like a tidal wave. She gagged, and retched, struggling to keep it in. She turned her head. "There must be some mistake," she muttered, trying to convince herself that her eyes were playing tricks on her. Perhaps she was more tired than she realised. "I need to go to sleep. It'll be different after I've rested my eyes," she told herself. Deep down, she suspected that it wouldn't be the case, but out of desperation, she forced herself to her bed, though not before locking the doors behind her. She took out a bulb from the hallway, then smashed it inside a towel, before scattering across the floor; just to be sure that she wasn't attacked in her sleep. Whatever sleep she could get. "This day can't get any worse," she muttered.

Chapter Fifteen

Did she realise that she had jinxed herself? Not straight away. As she laid on her bed, echoing the last thing she spoke, she let out an inward groan. Things could always get worse, and in her line of work, that should have been a bit of a clue. Her eyes turned towards the door. Her heart beat loud and heard, threatening to break out of her chest with each beat.

The external door slammed hard against a surface. She couldn't make out if it was slammed open, or slammed shut, but the sound of doors slamming was distinctive and memorable. "I know where you are! Come on out! We have the guy!" the familiar voice called out. She knew that voice from anywhere, half asleep or wide awake. It was the distinct sound of Mark, calling out her name. If they had caught the guy, why was it done so quickly? The hair on her arms fought against her. Something wasn't right. She thought back to the image. Her gut tightened. Was he really the killer, and had been playing her the whole time. His face reflecting in the window had shaken her to the core. But it still made no sense to her. Why would he do this?

She decided to call for the captain. It seemed like the best logical move. She kept her tone low, so that no one could hear her.

She dialled in the number and waited.

"Kate? Do you know what time it is? What is wrong?"

He sounded half asleep. Definitely not the sound of someone who had just caught a killer. Her eyes darted back to the screen, where Mark's face filled the screen. "I know who the killer is. You need to come and get me, now."

"What's wrong?" The captain asked. "Who is it?"

"It's Mark!" she whispered. "And he is right outside my door."

That jolted him awake. She could hear the springs bounce from his mattress. "I am on my way. Get to the bathroom, and use the exit I told you about. When you get there, stay put."

Mark was still outside, hammering ono one of the
doors. He hadn't reached her door yet. But he was
getting close.

She inched herself towards the floor, avoiding the
windows and doorways and headed for the
bathroom. As much as she wanted to grab the coffee
machine, she reassured herself that she can always
come back for it later. If not, well... it was the perfect
excuse to get the newer model--if she survives, that
is.
"Come on out. Let's talk!" Mark called out again.
She held her breath, and against her better
judgement, she made her way to the front door to
peer through the peephole. Mark was two door
down, and wearing black. Almost hidden in the
darkened hallway, his voice echoed through the
building like an empty shell.

Then, as though he sensed her, he moved towards
the next door. One door down. She was running out
of time. She reached for her gun and made her way
to the bathroom, opening the hatch beneath the mat
like she was instructed. She wont go yet, she told
herself . She will wait until the last possible
moment. If she can get a shot in, all the better.

After not opening the door, his tone hardened and
an aggressive edge to it. "I guess you know it was me

then," he called out, clearly hoping to bait her out. "I knew that you were too quiet. It was those photographs, wasn't it? You found something in one of those bloody pictures. What was it? My face? The office? Or was it the reflection you fixated on for the rest of the journey home. I hope you know," he said, not letting up. "The home invasion was not personal. I just needed something to get the others out of the way. This way, we won't be disturbed and I can have you to myself."

The restraint she had to take not to reply or call him something her mother would blush at, almost astonished her. She grit her teeth, using every fiber of her being to keep quiet. She cocked her gun, pointing it squarely at the door. All he had to do was walk up to it, and she would shoot. Maybe even get a headshot. She sniggered to herself. It worked on Call of Duty, didn't it? Hesitating, she inched back towards the bathroom. The hatch, still wide open, ready for her to take a trip down the slide. Though it wouldn't be for her, she decided. She grabbed her phone, and messaged the captain her plan. She was going to lure him inside, then push him down the hole. Hopefully, land him directly in front of the armed officers who would be waiting - and pointing their guns at him.

She squeezed out a bottle of soap over the titled floor in the bathroom and shoved the rug to one side. Then, she picked up a large shampoo bottle, aiming it directly at the door. She held her breath. Aiming, she was good at. Throwing... not so much. Giving it everything she had, she launched the tresemme at the door. The banging of the next door stopped. Footsteps echoed towards her. "This plan better work," she told herself, suddenly very aware that she was alone.

"What made you do it?" Kate called out, gripping the handle of her gun with everything she had. "Why did you send me half of the heart?!"
His cold laugh echoed in the hallway, and the hotel room door slammed open. That sound again. She held her position. Her body shook.
"Why?" he demanded with a laugh. "Because it was the only way to get your attention? What's good about a fake heart when I can give you the real thing?!"
"The real thing? You killed someone!" she screamed back. She watched as his shadow stretched across the hallway floor. He stood in the doorway, with his body filling the frame.
"Yes, well. He was already dying, and he was an organ donor. What better person to donate it to?"
Her eyes widened. "The person who needed it!"
He took a step into the hallway. The bulb glass crunched beneath his feet. He let out a low chuckle.

The type of chuckle that made her heart beat faster. It did the same now, and a chill ran down her spine. "We did need it, Kate. You wouldn't have seen me without it."

All this for her attention. It made her sick. "I saw you," she told him in a near whisper. "I always saw you. But now, I see you as something else--someone else. After what you have done, I can never be with you."

"Aw, pet," he replied with a smirk. He turned towards the bathroom, where she was standing, with the hatch hidden behind her. "You don't have much of a choice."

He raised his gun, smirking. "You and me, until death."

"Don't..." she pleaded quietly.

He scowled. "Don't? Don't tell me "Don't"!" he snapped. He pulled the trigger. She screamed, feeling the bullet whiz past her. Pain shot through her head. She raised her hand. The bullet grazed her, taking off a piece of her ear. She glared back at him. Then, swung her leg out from beneath him, and watched as he dived head first into the hatch. He screamed, blocking the slide with his feet. He aimed up between his legs, pointing his gun at her with a snarl. "Wrong choice!" Then, fired at her. She screamed, feeling hot searing heat pierce her stomach. She collapsed to the floor, and watched as he fell deeper down the slide.

Kate crawled over to the kitchen, and reached up to push the button on her coffee machine. The captain's voice called out to her, dripping with concern. "Kate? Are you alright?"

She grunted, as she shuffled back towards the hatch. "Not really," she told him loudly. "I'm missing a piece and I've got a hole in a couple of places."

"You've been hit?!" His voice was shrill. A cold laugh echoed through the slide, before being abruptly cut off. "Shut it!" the captain snapped aggressively. "I'll be dealing with you later." he let out a sigh. "Paramedics are on the way up. Which room are you in?"

She frowned and glanced at the still open door. "Twenty three," she replied.

"All right. Hold tight."

She let out a nervous laugh. "I don't think I'm gonna make it, Captain."

The slide fell silent for a moment, before three men rushed through the door. "We're here cap!" one called out, holding the first aid bag.

"How bad is it?" the captain replied.

The paramedic frowned, assessing the wounds. "She'll make it, but she has lost a lot of blood. We need to get her to the hospital now."

"Not without my coffee," she muttered.

The paramedic frowned, and sent his partner to go look in the kitchen, before returning with the full pot of coffee and her favourite mug. "Do you want the machine too?"

She thought about it, before finally shaking her head. "No," she replied weakly. "If I survive this, I'll buy myself another."

Epilogue

Kate placed the neatly folded pile of clothes into her bag. The captain was standing by the door, watching with a small smile. It had been a week since she had been shot, and now she was finally allowed to go home. Well, at least, what was left of it.

She turned back towards the Captain, frowning. "Wait, what happened with Mark?" she asked. "Why did he do what he did?"

The Captain sat down on the bed beside her, his expression softened.

"Jealousy," he stated, shrugging his shoulders. "You have so many friends, he wanted to be noticed. But if he had spent less time obsessing over you, and actually speaking to you, he'd have known that he was already noticed. But... he didn't."

She frowned. "But, why didn't I see it?"

"He was clever. He placed the parcel on your desk when he came in, making sure everyone else was grabbing coffee. So, there was no one to notice him doing anything. Then, being the first one to see your reaction. He then made sure that he was there at the right place and right time to be there for you. He insisted on being on the case. That way, he can spend more time with you, and keep an eye on the investigation."

She sighed, ducking her head. "I feel so stupid." She paused again, her frown deepened. "But my house... he couldn't have done that. He was with me the whole time."

He nodded. "Yeah, he had help. Remember those homeless kids outside your house, and outside the bakery that night?"

She nodded. "He said he needed to give them a warning not to hang about."

The Captain shook his head. "He bribed them to destroy your house, in exchange for housing and a comfortable lifestyle."

"Oh... What happened to them?"

"They have probation. And since he never actually followed through on his promise, they were happy to give up his name."

Kate looked around the room, realising how much she had taken for granted.

"He's going away for a long time," he promised.

She sighed again and nodded. "All right."

"Oh yeah," he gasped. "I almost forgot!"

She watched as he slipped his hand into his inside coat pocket.

"I found this on him. I guess he was hoping to look like a saviour?"

She lowered her gaze to his open palm and gasped. "My mum's necklace!" she cried. She threw her arms around his neck, hugging him tightly. "Thank you!" she said, whispering tearfully into his ear.

He cleared his throat, and fastened his coat with his free hand.

Finally, he stood up, and reached for her hand. "Are you ready?" he asked.

She nodded and hauled the bag over her shoulder, wincing slightly.

He held out his hand, smirking. "Oh no you don't. You need to get your strength back. I'm taking your bag. Besides, when we get back, there's a surprise waiting for you."

She frowned, looking at him sceptically. "Cap, what did you do?"

He laughed. "Stop calling me Cap. We're off duty. How many times do I have to tell you? Call me Cage."

She blushed and nodded. "Alright. Cage." She thought for a moment. There was something funny about saying his name, that gave her a little spark of anticipation; like saying a swear for the first time. "What did you do?"

He laughed again. "You will find out when I get you home."

The journey wasn't as long as she expected. After talking about what food she was missing, and the first thing she wanted to do, he nodded and smiled. She placed the key into the hole, turning it hesitantly before stepping into the hallway, unsure of what she would find.

The hallway carpet had been straightened out. She reached for the light switch, unsure. It wouldn't work before. She took a deep breath, and tried anyway, gasping as the room lit up. "You fixed my light?" she asked.

"Keep going," he insisted with a chuckle.

She led the way to the living-room. The memory of the destruction lingered in her mind like a bad dream. She pushed the living door open, holding her breath, unsure of what she would find.

"Surprise!"

A group of her colleagues jumped out from behind the sofa. Then, Cage gestured for her to sit down. She laughed and obeyed. "Thanks everyone!" she gasped, looking around. Everything was fixed. The windows were replaced, the furniture was restored, and her clothes and drawers were back into their rightful place.

Tears stung her eyes, grateful for the friends that she had. She really had been blessed.

"We have one more thing for you," Cage called out, his voice coming from the kitchen. She turned towards the door, licking her lips nervously. They had done so much already.

As Cage re-entered the living room, he revealed a brand new coffee machine.

"It isn't!" she gasped, tears threatening to fall again.

"It is," he told her. "We all pitched in and bought you a new coffee machine."

Liz stepped out from the crowd, pointing towards it gingerly. "It's the newest model."

"You guys!" Kate sobbed. "Thank you! I love you guys!"

Other books written by this author

Standalone Books:

The Last Gift

Grieving in Blood

The Feathered Accomplice

Series

The Dark Queen:
The Storm Within

A Holiday Mystery:
Book 1 - A Murder in Benidorm

COMING SOON

A Holiday Mystery
Book 2 - Dead in Turkey
Book 3 - Deadly Dancing in Morocco
Book 4 - A Body in Paris
Book 5 - Lost in NY City

The Dark Queen
Eye of the Storm
Ruler of the Ocean

My Heartless Valentine

My Heartless Valentine

Copyright © 2023 Reflective Line Publishing
All rights reserved

First Edition, 2023
Published by Reflective Line Publishing

www.reflectivelinepublishing.wordpress.com

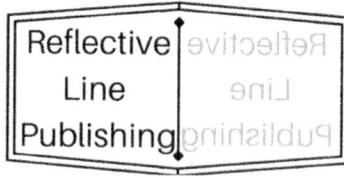

Reflective
Line
Publishing

125

Printed in Great Britain
by Amazon